The train became a vehicle of death...

Karen had been sleeping in her compartment when she suddenly felt a massive jolt...and heard the awful sounds of wrenching metal. Now she gazed in numb horror from her window. The train had derailed!

Sick with fear, she hastened to the door and jumped to safety. Her eyes quickly scanned the throng of terrified passengers. But Stuart—the handsome stranger she'd dined with that evening—was nowhere to be seen.

Her last thought as she watched the train burst into flames was of Stuart. Was he still inside...trapped?

Chance Encounter

by JOEL AUDRENN

MYSTIQUE BOOKS

TORONTO·LONDON·NEW YORK
HAMBURG·AMSTERDAM·STOCKHOLM

CHANCE ENCOUNTER/first published May 1981

ISBN 0-373-50128-5

PRINTED IN CANADA

Chapter 1

Karen Stockwell felt a surge of relief when the taxi from the airport finally made its way through the heavy traffic of Paris. She was home again. Although her business trip to Oslo had taken only three days to complete, it felt as if she had been gone for weeks. To save time she had instructed the driver to take the expressway that encircled the heart of Paris; it wasn't the straightest line to her destination, but it was certainly preferable to the snarls and jams of city traffic.

The tension and weariness she hadn't dared permit before now settled on her. It had been her first business experience totally on her own, and she only hoped that her employer, Franz Kleimer, realized just how expensive everything in Oslo was. When he'd sent her off with the company Eurocard and more than five hundred dollars' worth of Norwegian cash, she had been taken aback. It had seemed an extravagant amount of money to her for two nights in a hotel, taxi fares and a few meals out. However, she soon learned that the man had been right. Yes, she still had some cash left over, but not very much. The expensive restaurants had honored her credit card, but the moderately priced ones seldom had.

She leaned back against the seat and closed her eyes for a moment. Karen had been entirely too excited about being entrusted to handle the arrangements for the exhibition all on her own to be able to sleep well; and the noises and different rhythm of a strange city hadn't helped. Nonetheless, she had pulled it off, and she knew that Franz would be pleased with her. Realizing that the cabby was turning off the expressway, she opened her eyes and enjoyed the sight of familiar buildings on the Avenue Foch. Soon they would be at the Place Charles de Gaulle, circling the Arc de Triomphe, and almost at the Kleimer Gallery.

When the car finally pulled up in front of the gallery on the Rue du Faubourg St. Honoré, one of the most elegant addresses in the city, she pulled her heavy winter coat around her and got out of the taxi. The driver lifted her suitcase out of the front of the taxi while she counted off the bills to pay him. It was much colder in Paris than it had been in Oslo, and the streetlights were already on.

Smiling faintly, she thanked the driver and lugged her suitcase to the large glass doors of the fashionable art gallery. As always she was dazzled by the immaculately clean glass, which now showed a gleaming reflection of the snowplowed street.

Stepping inside, she slipped her suitcase behind the untended desk of the gallery's receptionist, Jenny, and looked around with tired gratitude. The placard before the large room on the right read: Crowds in the Summer Hell of the South of France. Through the door she could see about twenty people wandering around the room, leaning forward to inspect some detail of a painting or standing back with a loose fist to achieve a telescope effect. Karen recognized some of them as regular customers or frequent browsers and assumed that Jenny was probably with the others, blocked from view because of her petite frame.

To Karen's left were two smaller rooms, which Franz Kleimer referred to as the "bric-a-brac suites," housing a few genuine treasures surrounded by accumulations of early junk that nonetheless sold very well.

The security guard, a large bearlike fellow, lumbered into the foyer, recognized her and acknowledged her return with a forefinger raised to the brim of his cap. A retired policeman, the guard never did understand why anyone would want to buy any of the paintings or objets d'art but knew better than to say anything in front of Mr. Kleimer himself.

A few seconds later Jenny entered the foyer, patiently answering questions put to her by a plump dowager. "Oh, excuse me, Mrs. Bonneville...I'll be right back."

She crossed over to Karen with an expectant smile. "How did it go?"

"Quite well, I think," she answered, taking off her imitation fur hat and slipping out of her woolen coat. "Is himself upstairs?"

"Yes, and rather worried about you. We'd expected you to return more than an hour ago." Jenny took Karen's hat and coat and folded them neatly on the seat of the chair behind the desk.

"We were delayed in Oslo...something about the caterers bringing the wrong meals to the plane, or maybe it was because they hadn't brought enough. It doesn't matter. But I didn't think it warranted a long-distance call to let Franz know."

Jenny laughed understandingly. "While I can't say he's France's answer to Scrooge, still he's mindful of every penny that's spent needlessly."

"Miss? Oh, miss?" The robust woman customer was becoming visibly impatient.

"I've got to go," Jenny whispered. "Talk to you later."

Karen watched the slim girl return to the customer, then climbed the broad staircase to the second floor, which housed Franz Kleimer's office as well as the living quarters for him and his wife. Before he had converted the downstairs to a gallery, the place had been a very ornate townhouse; the rooms were large, and each had its own fireplace. The paned windows were almost ten feet high, with short balconies that overlooked the busy street below. Each room was decorated in the style of Louis XVI, with white walls and gilded moldings to enhance the elegance of the furnishings. While this was not the sort of decor Karen would ever want to live with, she could still appreciate its beauty and the craftsmanship of the early cabinetmakers.

At the top of the stairs she rapped lightly on a door before turning the handle and entering. "Who is it?" Franz called out.

"Karen," she answered, approaching the far side of the room where Franz sat in his wheelchair with his back to her.

Gnarled, arthritic hands worked the wheels, and he turned to greet her. "At last! I've been worried about you, dear girl. But here you are now, safe and sound." He smiled broadly, his gray mustache a bristling awning over his teeth. "Now, tell me—how did it go!"

She lowered herself onto a French rococo side chair and placed her handbag on the floor next to the carved leg. "I am pleased to report that Mr. Lund finally acquiesced. At first he kept making noises that I'd wasted my time and your money, that there was no way he'd consent to lending us the exhibit."

Franz nodded sagely, his dark brown eyes narrowing. "But then you gave him my little speech I rehearsed you in?"

"Yes and no," she replied cautiously. Just then Franz Kleimer's wife, Ilse—a highly attractive, mature woman who carried more weight than was fashionable—entered the room. Karen began to stand, but Ilse gestured to her to remain seated.

"What do you mean by 'yes and no'?" Franz leaned forward in his chair, his dark eyes registering instant alarm.

Karen took a deep breath. "I thought about the speech all during the plane trip to Oslo, and since this was my initiation, I decided it wouldn't do. I'd only bungle everything, and you'd be disappointed, if not angry, and I'd never get another chance."

"Why do you say that, Karen?" Ilse asked, seating herself nearby.

"Because," Karen began, looking the older woman straight in the eyes, "it was Franz's speech—not mine. He could say those words and be successful because Franz is known; people already respect his opinions and his manner of doing business. But for me, a fledgling, to say such things would only seem impudent and out of place."

Ilse glanced at her husband, arching her eyebrows as if to convey Karen was right. Franz Kleimer was not accustomed to having his instructions countermanded, yet he had enormous faith in his wife's judgment. "Go on, my dear."

"Well, what I did was to take the nucleus of the information and put it into my own words. I was candid about this being my first attempt to negotiate an exhibition and hoped that Mr. Lund would understand how important it was to me to be successful. In short I appealed to his chivalry first. Then I told him what Franz's opinions were—not mine, but Franz's— and said I hoped that he would see the merit in the reasoning."

The old man's hands clenched the metal arm of his chair. "But he *did* consent, didn't he? Isn't that what you said?"

"Oh, yes," she answered, smiling to herself. "He was a little annoyed that a young woman should be sent on a man's job, but little by little he realized that I knew what I was talking about."

"Thus earning his respect on your own," Ilse interjected.

"Especially when he wanted to use TransEuro Shipping as a means of getting the paintings here, and I told him that they were not only overpriced, but that they had lost two containers from a circulating exhibit from New York's Museum of Modern Art."

"How do you know that?" Franz inquired curiously.

"It was in the trade news last week."

"Hmm. I don't recall seeing that," the old man admitted.

"Neither had Mr. Lund; he explained that he was a few weeks behind in his reading. But I did, and it seemed to impress him."

"What happened to the containers?" Ilse asked, barely suppressing a smile.

"Oh," Karen replied, shrugging, "they were found a few days later. They had been shipped to Belgium instead of Holland, that's all. But it did mean that the exhibit couldn't open when it was supposed to, and that cost the museum some money and embarrassment."

Franz's hands slapped his knee lightly. "Very well. The main thing is that you succeeded. We can now proceed with having our announcements printed up and sent to our regular patrons, the ads in the newspapers and—" He stopped in midsentence and looked at Karen carefully. "Do you suppose we could get some free publicity out of this on TV? You know, something like cultural exchange information?"

"Probably, but not immediately," she answered, hunching her shoulders to stretch out the tension in her muscles. "All I want to do right now is go home, take a long hot bath, have a light supper and go straight to bed."

"Poor child," Ilse commiserated. "You must be exhausted."

"Uh, well," Franz said hesitantly, "I hate to tell you this, Karen, but we have a small problem."

She became instantly wary; whenever Franz referred to a "small problem," it was usually a very large one and more often than not one that ended up in her lap. She'd been with the gallery for more than two years, straight out of art-history classes in college, and she'd come to know the old man quite well. Beneath his gruff exterior he was a good man; however, it never seemed to occur to him that even young people had their limits in physical endurance. Instead he took the attitude that

only he, since he was crippled, tired easily; anyone
under the age of thirty was expected to have sufficient
stamina for a marathon.

Karen waited for him to tell her just what his minor
problem was, noticing that half-guilty glance he sent in
Ilse's direction.

"You see," he began carefully, "it's about the
Sumerian mask—the one that was discovered in a
pawnbroker's cellar in Nice." His gray eyebrows drew
together as he obviously composed his remarks swiftly. "If you'll recall, it was an antique that had
been stolen a century ago by a digger on an archae-
ological site in Mesopotamia. It was sold, stolen again
and has turned up dozens of times, only to be stolen and
sold anew."

"I'm familiar with the mask," Karen admitted
guardedly.

"Good. Well, that old goat Cagliani has had it in his
possession for at least eight months. He refused to lend
it to a museum for exhibition, insisted he'd never let it
out of his sight."

Franz Kleimer ran his bony hand through his thinning
gray hair, a gesture Karen knew well as a tip-off that he
was trying to convince her to do something she would
prefer not to.

"Whatever his reasons," the old man resumed, "he's
now prepared to hold a private auction for it. Only
about a dozen handpicked buyers have been invited to
his villa in Cimiez near Nice."

"When did this come up?" Ilse asked with open
curiosity.

He waved her question aside. "I only received the invitation in yesterday's mail."

"And you want me to go to the auction," Karen anticipated. "When is it?"

"The viewing is tomorrow, probably after one of his ostentatious luncheons."

"Tomorrow!" Karen's dark blue eyes widened. "But I can't possibly do it, Franz! I'm bone weary now.... I wouldn't be able to keep my eyes open.... I'd probably fall asleep at the table with my face in the soup!"

"Don't be silly, my dear," he argued. "You're young and in perfect health—there's not a reason in the world to pamper yourself! What will you do when you get to be my age if you go on like that?"

"I won't reach your age if you keep overworking me," she reasoned tartly.

Ilse leaned forward. "What about Eric, darling? Why don't you send him instead?"

"No, no," Franz objected, drumming his fingers on the arm of his wheelchair. "Cagliani won't have Eric anywhere near his place. He's afraid of Eric's well-known skepticism—that Eric will look for indications of forgery and scare off his prospective buyers."

Karen let her head drop, pressing her fingers to her temples. Eric Guzman was the gallery's authority on retainer for major buys. He was the most knowledgeable man Karen had ever met, but she had to agree that he frequently was too cautious. "So that leaves me," she said quietly.

"I'm afraid so," Franz said. "I hate to do this to you, Karen, but there's no choice."

"I see."

"Now it's all been taken care of, my dear. You're already packed, and you'll be tucked in bed by midnight."

"I dread the idea of getting on another plane," she said.

He wheeled over to her and patted her arm gently. "You won't have to. On such short notice there wasn't a single seat on any flight, so Jenny reserved a sleeping compartment on the Trans Europe Express, leaving at six-thirty tonight."

"Are you absolutely certain that Eric wouldn't be the better choice?" Karen asked, hoping to turn the old man around. "He's far better qualified than I am."

Franz shook his head. "Of course he is; but as I said, Cagliani won't let him near the auction."

"But I hardly know anything about the mask of Lugalki, only something I once read in an art review, a few photographs I've seen and a cast of it I saw years ago at the Guimet Museum. How will I know it isn't a fake?"

The old man *tsk*ed. "I've thought it all through, my dear. I've put together a dossier about the mask from my personal files. You'll have plenty of time on the train to go over the information." He reached inside his jacket and pulled out an envelope. "There are three checks in here made out for what I believe the lowest possible price will be, the next lowest and my maximum bid. If I had unlimited resources, I'd pay anything to own the mask of Lugalki—but I'm just not that wealthy. You're my only hope, Karen. You must do this for me!"

"It really means that much to you, Franz?" she asked, her eyes meeting the art dealer's.

"I've coveted it all my life, Karen. What I'm prepared to pay for it, admittedly, probably isn't enough. But I'm counting on the short notice to preclude some of the millionaire bidders from attending. If that happens, we have a fighting chance of buying the mask." His voice trailed off, and he hunched forward as if overcome with emotion.

"All right, Franz, I'll do my best. Where's your dossier?"

"To the left of my desk, right on top."

She got to her feet with effort and crossed over to the huge ornate desk. There was something almost ominous about the bulging manila folder, as if it might contain secrets never meant to be seen by anyone. She picked it up almost gingerly. "All right, Franz, but you know this is a sacrifice, and I wouldn't do it for anyone else."

"Of course, my dear, and I truly appreciate it," he replied.

"Enough to give me a few days off when I return?"

Both Ilse and Franz laughed. "I'll see to it that he does," Ilse guaranteed, rising from her chair to walk Karen to the door. "You'll be in Nice tomorrow, rested and restored. You can either come back tomorrow night or wait till Friday. Either way, after you've reported to us what happened, we won't expect you in the gallery until Wednesday of next week. I promise."

"Wednesday?" Franz repeated plaintively, half in question.

"Wednesday," Ilse confirmed with a sly wink at Karen.

Smiling, Karen nodded her thanks to Mrs. Kleimer, and clutching the folder and her handbag, she left the room.

Chapter 2

Regardless of Franz's statement about her being already packed, Karen took a taxi back to her apartment. Usually she took the subway to the Place de Clichy, then walked the few blocks to the Rue Chaptal. However, not only was she too tired to lug a suitcase on the subway and then walk, but there was very little time before she had to catch the train.

She needed fresh underwear, of course. But what Franz hadn't taken into consideration was that Nice was a winter resort—the weather would be the opposite of what it had been in Oslo! Karen hadn't said anything to him only because it seemed pointless under the circumstances. Then, too, she would have to cancel her dinner engagement with Maria and George Ferrier, much as she didn't want to. They were her foster parents; they had raised her from the age of five, and had always been more than merely kind to Karen. She loved them as much as she could ever love her "real" parents. Even when they ceased to receive any government assistance for her support—when she reached the age to get a job—they insisted that she continue to live with them and get a college education.

Once back in her apartment, Karen put the kettle on for tea and then phoned the Ferriers. They were disappointed but understood, and they set another date for the following week. She hung up, glancing out the window, and noticed that a light snow was falling. "Let's hope it doesn't get any worse," she muttered to herself, then hefted her suitcase onto the couch and opened it. By then the kettle was whistling, and throwing off her shoes, she padded to the efficiency kitchen to fix her tea.

Interrupted by the ringing of the telephone, she crossed the small living room to the secondhand end table and picked up the receiver. "Hello?"

There was a short silence. "Karen—it's me, Alex."

Her hands grew cold at the sound of his voice, and she could feel the pulse pounding in her temples. "How dare you call me," she said slowly, unable to conceal the outrage she felt.

"Look, I know I did a rotten thing to you, but I need you, Karen. Let's not forget how much we once meant to each other!"

A derisive smile crossed Karen's oval face. "The operative word is 'once,' Alex. You walked out on me, remember? Said you'd met a lonely divorcée with money to burn, if I recall correctly." Even though her words dripped with sarcasm, she couldn't quell the inner churning that his voice evoked.

"It was stupid of me, darling, I know I hurt you badly, but I've now seen how very wrong I was. It's you I love and always will!"

Her imagination envisioned what his expression

would be right then. The dark unruly hair falling over his broad forehead, those brown eyes imploring, head cocked to one side in supplication.... Oh, yes, she knew Alex and all his wiles all too well. "Three months ago you thought you could live very nicely without me," she reminded him pointedly.

"I have to see you," he insisted urgently. "I've been trying to call you for days, but you're never home."

Karen didn't bother to tell him that she'd been out of the country; let him wonder where she had been. "I've been busy," she answered shortly.

"What about this evening," he cajoled. "We could have dinner together—try to pick up where we left off."

"No, Alex. I've got other plans for tonight. And frankly as far as you're concerned, I'm always busy. I'm going to hang up now, Alex. You'll only be wasting your time if you ever try to phone me again."

"No! Please! I—"

She didn't hear the rest but carefully put the receiver back in its cradle. Still in something of a daze, she stood staring at the telephone, then glanced at her hands. They were trembling slightly, but she was regaining control of herself. Three months was a long time, and although the way Alex had terminated their engagement had broken her heart, she at least had had the satisfaction of knowing that she was well out of it. Any man who could just dump his fiancée of more than a year after all the plans they had made was not the man she wanted to spend the rest of her life with. He had met a woman with some money, who bought him presents, and like some gigolo in a B movie he had decided that she was better game than Karen. Well, he had made his decision.... Let him live with it.

Angrily she returned to the kitchen and resumed what she had been doing. That Alex still had the power to upset her, to hurt her, irked Karen considerably. But she had been firm, resolute, and she was proud of herself.

THE SNOW FELL SLOWLY, barely heavier than the night air, as the taxi let her off in front of the train station with only minutes to spare. She raced through the station to the platform where the Trans Europe Express waited, carrying her own suitcase to save time and hampered by it as she tried to get past the clusters of people saying their goodbyes. Each compartment of the first-class cars had an individual door; some were open, with passengers boarding quickly, and others were closed, with the travelers leaning over the lowered windows calling out last-minute farewells or just observing the scene.

The attendant on board took Karen's suitcase as she climbed up, then showed her to her sleeping compartment off the narrow passageway. "Will you need to be awakened before we reach Nice?" he asked courteously.

"I'd appreciate it," she said, knowing that as tired as she was, she might sleep through. "Perhaps you would bring breakfast at the same time—some cereal and tea with milk would do nicely."

"I'll make a note of it," the porter said, pulling out a small pad and pencil. "Do you prefer to make up your berth yourself, or shall I come back later and attend to it?"

The train began to move, and Karen steadied herself by resting a hand against the wall of her compartment. The air in the small room was acrid, smelling of steam and metal, and she could hardly wait to open the window. "You take care of it, please," she answered. "I'll probably want some dinner later."

He shook his head as he put the notebook back in his pocket. "I don't think there are many seats left for the first sitting."

"I prefer the second anyway."

The man nodded pleasantly. "You're traveling alone?"

"Yes, but please...if it's at all possible, I'd prefer to eat alone, as well. I don't feel up to pleasant, polite chit-chat."

"Certainly, miss, I'll do the very best I can," he said, accepting the large tip she handed him, then turning away up the corridor.

She closed the narrow door, pulled off her boots and sat down heavily on the small built-in couch that would convert to her bed later. Leaning over, she lowered the window on the outside door, hoping to let in some air, then sat back and rested her head against the wall. It had been a very long day, and her feet felt as if they'd been packed in cement. Karen sighed heavily, wiggled her toes, then slipped her heavy winter coat off. She reached over for her briefcase and took out the file on the mask of Lugalki.

As was to be expected, Franz's dossier was a mess of wrinkled carbons, clippings from magazines and newspapers yellowed with age, and photocopies of documentation reports from sundry museums over the years. A few black-and-white photographs were included, along with some color pictures taken from magazine articles about the mask. She began to read from the top, seeking any tips on fakes or on how to verify the authenticity of the mask that was to be auctioned the next day.

Finally she came across a memo from Eric Guzman to Franz Kleimer dated that very morning:

The mask that Cagliani is trying to sell is nothing more than a superb copy in solid gold—which is worth its weight in today's inflated market and nothing more. I have it on good authority that Cagliani has already sold two other "originals" of the mask, and the auction in Cimiez is little more than a hoax. Granted, some damn fool will fall for it the same as the two previous buyers were duped, but I warn you against being the one who is taken.

"Oh, no," Karen groaned aloud. What was she supposed to do now? Eric knew much, much more about such things than she did.... How was she to know if Eric was right, or if Cagliani had the real mask? She couldn't very well ask the man if he was ripping people off! On the other hand if the mask was genuine, failing to bid on it could cost her her job! Word would be bound to get back to Franz that she'd shown up but hadn't made any offer. "Damn, damn, damn," she said under her breath, wishing for a second that she had gone to work for the civil service instead—a nice, dull, steady job with no major decisions on her shoulders.

Karen tossed the file to one side and stared out the window at the scenery whizzing by. She noticed that the snow was beginning to accumulate on her window. By the light cast from her compartment she could see that it was much heavier here than it had been in Paris.

The porter in the passageway was calling out that the next stop would be Laroche-Migennes, but she barely heard him. Her mind drifted back to the phone call from

Alex earlier. "I'll always love you, darling—we'll be together forever!" Karen could still see his face, so serious, as he took her in his strong arms. They had gone on an excursion to the palace at Versailles early that summer, nearly stunned by the opulence and splendor of the former residence of Louis XIV, the most elaborate royal palace in the entire world. They had toured the magnificent gardens, holding hands and laughing; and in the late afternoon, a bit pink from the unaccustomed sunshine, they had taken the bus back to Paris.

It had been a perfect day, and she had loved Alex so very much. He was everything she had ever dreamed of: handsome, virile and strong. When he had taken her home that evening, he had proposed to her, and with tears of joy she had accepted. His kiss had been fiercely passionate, proclaiming Karen as his own at last. That had been the happiest period of her life, even though her foster parents didn't seem too keen about the marriage.

"I love you...I love you...I love you...." In her head his words echoed the sound of the train's wheels on the track over and over again. But he had walked out on her for an older woman who spent her money lavishly. Alex had been bought; it was as simple as that.

Karen's gaze shifted from the driving snow beyond. The countryside could no longer be discerned in the darkness, and her eyes focused on her reflection in the window. The effect was dramatic. Her high cheekbones seemed to be more defined, the planes of her face accentuated. Her mouth, already a bit wider than she liked, seemed fuller, more anxious to be kissed. The window didn't give an accurate reflection, she noticed, since her large blue eyes seemed brown, and her tawny blond hair had red tones that didn't exist.

Perhaps, she thought, *if I really looked like this, Alex wouldn't have left.* But, of course, she knew that wasn't true. He had wanted money, security.... What a woman looked like obviously didn't matter much; what she stood for, her character, had nothing to do with his decision. Money. *What a stupid waste*, she concluded, then glanced down at her watch just as the porter was making his way back, announcing the second sitting for dinner.

Opening her handbag, she took out a comb and ran it through her shoulder-length hair, then slid open her compartment door and headed toward the dining car just a few steps behind the attendant in her car.

When they reached the last connecting bellows of the two cars ahead, a steward greeted her in the subdued light of the dining car. He exchanged a questioning glance with the porter as if to verify that this was the woman who had tipped so well for her privacy. "Miss Stockwell?" he asked in a polite tone.

Karen nodded as she glanced down the dining car nearly packed to capacity with animated, cheerful passengers. Most of them, she knew, were going to Nice to escape the harshness of the winter in Paris, and there was a festive, holiday mood in the air.

"I'm terribly sorry, Miss Stockwell," the steward said, "but your request was among the last we received." He gestured broadly to the passengers as if all of them had boarded the train days ahead of her. "The best I can do is seat you at table twenty-four. At least there'll be only one other passenger instead of three."

In a momentary pique she wondered if the porter was going to refund the tip she'd given him, but she swiftly realized she was being childish. What difference did another passenger make? Would industry come to a crushing halt...the world stop spinning on its axis? Smiling wanly, she said, "It doesn't really matter all that much."

The steward bowed stiffly, then straightened almost with a ballet dancer's *port de bras* as he led her to her table. He turned toward the end of the car, then pulled her chair out for her. Seated on the opposite side was a man whom Karen guessed to be in his early thirties. He rose as she reached the table, and she was surprised at how tall he was.

"Good evening," he said with a cordial smile revealing strong, even teeth.

"Good evening," she responded as the steward seated her.

"I'm Stuart Macloud," he said, sitting down again.

Karen was pleased that he had a well-modulated speaking voice. "Karen Stockwell," she responded, leaning back as the waiter poured water into her glass. "Have you already ordered?" she inquired.

"No, I was informed that I'd have a dinner partner, so I thought it only courteous to wait." He handed her the menu, which he had propped against the saltshaker. "I'd like to make a suggestion if you won't think me too forward."

Karen looked into his clear hazel eyes, noticing the tiny laugh wrinkles at the corners. His features were more Anglo-Saxon than French, and then she remembered that his name wasn't French, either. His light brown hair was styled, not just barbered, and the gold signet ring he wore on the little finger of his left hand was obviously eighteen karat.

"Did you hear me?" he asked, his baritone voice politely curious.

"I'm sorry," she said with a little laugh. "My mind was wandering. You wanted to make a suggestion?"

"Yes." He gave her a lopsided smile as if to apologize beforehand. "I, well, I was expecting some old biddy to be seated across from me—the type who carried toy poodles in her handbag, if you know what I mean."

Amused, she tilted her head and waited for him to continue.

"That was the best I was hoping for," Stuart explained. "At worst, some old duffer who can't talk about anything except his days of military service."

Karen laughed. "You might have been better off," she said wryly. "I'm so whipped I doubt that I'll be much of a conversationalist . . . but I'm a darned good listener."

Stuart shook his head. "My point," he said slowly "is that I'm delighted to have a young, attractive dinner companion. And to pay homage to the fates who arranged it, I should very much like you to be my guest."

She began to protest, explaining that this was a business trip, and all her expenses would be charged back, but Stuart wouldn't hear of it. "May I order a drink for you—something to make us forget it's winter?"

Karen leaned back in her chair, looking at him and feeling very at ease in his company. "Having just returned from Oslo, only to find Paris even colder, I'd love one."

Stuart lifted his head to find their waiter, and Karen noticed that he had the bearing of a man accustomed to service of the highest order. Without his even raising a finger, the waiter responded to his glance instantly.

"The lady and I would like two American martinis on the rocks—made with vodka," he said, then looked at Karen to verify that his choice was acceptable. "Lemon twist or olive?"

"Twist."

"I'll have two olives but not in the drink—they take up too much room," he added, laughing, and watched the waiter's retreat.

"That's what I hate about martinis," Karen said. "They involve too many decisions. Gin or vodka, straight up or on the rocks, twist or olive.... That's why I usually only have a glass of sherry, if anything at all."

Stuart grinned. "Than aren't you glad we met tonight? I'll make all the decisions for you if you'll trust a stranger."

Under other circumstances Karen would have resented such a suggestion. She preferred to make her own choices. But Stuart had such an engaging air about him, such a pleasant manner, that she agreed. "I'll eat anything but raw oysters."

"Really? You're missing something wonderful then."

"Maybe. But slithery foods make me very queasy," she said, handing the menu back to him just as the waiter brought their cocktails.

"You said this is a business trip, and that you'd just returned from Oslo," Stuart remarked. "Does your business always have you traveling so much?"

Karen traced lines down the side of her frosted glass, hoping the powerful drink wouldn't knock her out in thirty seconds. "I work for the Kleimer Gallery and was just promoted to the position of Mr. Kleimer's personal assistant. There's an auction in Nice tomorrow, and I've been dispatched to represent the gallery."

"Really? How fascinating that must be. I suppose you mean the sale of the mask of Lugalki?"

Her blue eyes couldn't conceal her surprise. "But how did you know about it? Only a handful of people were invited!"

"Oh, I usually hear about all those sorts of things. But in truth, my father was one of those invited by Mr. Cagliani."

"Macloud," Karen said under her breath, trying to remember if she knew the name from somewhere.

Stuart watched her for a moment, then said, "Think in terms of oil tankers, and it'll come to you."

Her mouth fell agape for a second before she recovered her composure. "*The* Maclouds? Macloud Shipping in England?"

He nodded his affirmation. "Don't get any grandiose ideas, though. My father has me in and out of his will so often I sometimes wonder if his lawyers have a rubber stamp. You know, In or Out, depending on my dad's whim."

"Black sheep?"

He pulled a pack of cigarettes from his pocket, offered Karen one—which she declined—then lighted it. "Not in the usual sense. He insisted I abandon my hopes of becoming an attorney in order to come into the business with him. Since I knew that I wasn't a very good lawyer, I agreed. But every time I make a decision for the company, my dad countermands it—and then we have another donnybrook."

She smiled, trying to imagine what it would be like to work for one's father. "I suppose he just looks upon you as his little boy, instead of a grown-up. Do you like your work?"

"Most of the time," Stuart said, blowing smoke over her head. "I'm in the legal department, handling international law matters governing shipping lines. It's a lot better than trying to survive as a trial lawyer when you graduated from the bottom half of your class," he concluded dryly.

"I don't know if you're being serious or not, Stuart," Karen remarked perplexedly.

"Half and half," he answered with a twinkle in his hazel eyes. "Now, about you," Stuart said, swiftly changing the subject. "However did you come by the name Stockwell? You're obviously one hundred percent French—in fact, you remind me a great deal of Simone Signoret when she was your age. Married name?" He quickly glanced at her left hand.

"No. My father was English, but my mother was French. You're smiling," she commented. "Did I say something funny?"

"No, I'm merely surprised that two non-French-named people would be aboard this train, having dinner together, when it isn't the peak tourist season."

"It is unusual, I agree. And you, of course, are very British—right?"

"Wrong. My father is, of course, but my mother's an American."

"I can never understand that type of marriage," Karen said simply. "The English are so reserved, and the Americans so candid and extraverted."

"My mother refers to it as a balance of power," Stuart said lightly.

Karen looked at him, somewhat surprised by the warmth in his voice. "You love your mother a great deal, don't you?" she said.

"Not only love her but respect her, too. I think she knows more about the shipping business than my father, me and the late Onassis combined. She's a highly intelligent woman with an excellent sense of humor."

"Obviously where you get your own whimsical outlook."

His mouth curled in amusement. "Well, it wasn't from my dad, that's for sure! The only time I ever see him smile is when he's about to fire someone. I'd expect to see the Rock of Gibraltar having a good belly laugh before my father would."

"But you do love him, don't you?"

"If he'd let me," Stuart replied evenly. "Shall we have dinner?"

Realizing that the subject was unwelcome, Karen agreed and found herself watching this man in fascination as he ordered their dinner. Was his self-effacement only a ruse? He was handsome, educated and still quite young.... Surely he had a better opinion of himself than he was displaying. But it was none of her business. They'd have a pleasant dinner together, go their separate ways, and in the morning they'd disembark and never see one another again. Nonetheless, Karen knew that she liked Stuart Macloud, liked his combination of carefree and urbane traits. She hoped that when his father died, the last rubber stamp to be used would be In.

Chapter 3

By the time Karen got back to her compartment, it was far later than she had intended. But Stuart's charm and ebullience had been so much fun that she had totally forgotten how very tired she was. He had ordered scampi for them both, which was among the most expensive items on the menu, the dish was delicious and beautifully presented. Stuart's choice of wine had been perfect, and he had insisted that she have a liqueur after dinner. By the time they had said good-night, Karen was pleasantly mellow and ready for a good, dreamless sleep.

How lucky for her that her dinner companion had turned out to be such a likable fellow. He'd been keenly interested in the mask of Lugalki, so she had told him a little about its history. "He was a Sumerian prince of the second dynasty of Kish," Karen had explained. "The goldsmiths of Ur modeled the mask, it's believed."

"And it was used on the prince's sarcophagus presumably," Stuart had said.

"Yes, but it was stolen a hundred years ago from the excavations of Kulyab in Mesopotamia."

Stuart had cocked his head with an admiring look in his hazel eyes. "You're certainly well informed."

Karen laughed. "I brushed up before dinner."

"No—that is, maybe you did, but your retention is a strong sign of high intelligence. How unusual," he'd said, "to find beauty and brains in one woman."

"You're being a traditionalist," she'd chided lightly. "Now that more and more women have the opportunity for higher education, I don't think that old cliché will survive much longer."

"Touché. You're right, of course."

Later when Stuart had walked her back to her compartment, he'd stopped her at the door. She had hoped that he wouldn't make a pass, destroying her impressions of him. Instead he had looked down at her earnestly. "I'm in Paris frequently," he'd said. "May I call you the next time I'm there?"

"I'd like that."

"How can I reach you?" He'd asked, patting his pockets in search of paper and pen, then shrugging helplessly.

"I'm almost always at the gallery.... You can call me there."

"Kleimer, you said?"

She'd nodded, stepping inside. "Thanks for the lovely evening."

Slowly, almost hesitantly, Stuart had leaned over and kissed her on the cheek. "The pleasure was mine, Karen."

Now she watched him as he walked away down the narrow corridor, balancing against the swaying motion of the train like a sailor on high seas, then she slid her door closed. Locking it, she pulled the blind down, and then noting that the snow was coming in from her outside window, she moved to close it. Her bed was already made up and turned down, and her coat had been hung up neatly. She started to stifle a yawn but then decided she'd earned it.

Gazing out, she saw that there was practically a raging blizzard going on. Silently she hoped that it wouldn't affect her journey. The idea of being stuck on a train in the middle of nowhere held no appeal at all.

Karen opened her suitcase and removed her slippers, nightgown, robe and the kit containing her toothbrush and other articles. Yawning again, she was glad that she'd had the foresight to put those things on top so she didn't have to unpack totally. She eased out of her boots again, wishing she could soak her feet in Epsom salts, put on her slippers and sat down on the edge of the bed. The image of Stuart Macloud wouldn't leave her, so she decided to have a cigarette before getting ready for bed—a practice she rarely indulged in.

Propping up the pillows behind her, she recreated the dinner and her conversation with Stuart. Easygoing, self-assured, an avid listener—traits she rarely found among most of the young men she had met in her life. Alex had had them, too, she remembered, but they were a facade—a pose to lure his prey. Was Stuart also pretending? No, she doubted it. He was from a wealthy family and wouldn't need to resort to games. Why would he?

He had told her that he loved tennis and skiing—which she could easily believe from his trim physique—that he enjoyed theater and good books. They had found no end of things to talk about, interests they had in common. By the time their liqueurs were served, Karen had felt as if she'd known this man for a long time—except for the knowledge that he truly was a stranger to her, which added a dash of spice to the occasion. Not since Alex had she been so attracted to a man. *And that's something to bear in mind,* she warned herself solemnly. But if he had meant it about phoning her when next he was in Paris, there'd be time enough to decide if the similarities were coincidental or not. Perhaps he'd never call at all. Chance acquaintances, no matter how enjoyable, were frequently forgotten in the bustle of one's normal routine.

Karen watched the smoke from her cigarette curling upward and wondered what Stuart was doing at that moment. He'd probably ordered a large Scotch from the porter in car eleven. Just two cars away, she thought, and yet he might as well have been on a different continent.

She smiled to herself as she thought of how much fun she'd have next Thursday when she told her foster parents about having had dinner with the son of *the* Macloud family. Stuart had referred to his mother as Lady Macloud.... Did that mean that she was a countess or a marchioness? And was Stuart then a marquis or an earl? She didn't know very much about English peerage, but she assumed that the Maclouds weren't of royal lineage. It was far more likely that a title had been conferred; but still, how excited Maria and George would be! They led such ordinary, middle-class lives, that this event would give them something to talk about for weeks!

She ground out her cigarette, thinking of various

ways she would tell her foster parents about Stuart, then closed her eyes. In seconds she was fast asleep.

HER FIRST REACTION was to think that she'd been having a nightmare. She'd felt a massive jolt, and roused enough from her slumber to realize that she had fallen asleep with her clothes on. But this realization was succeeded instantly by an ominous swaying and the sounds of wrenching metal against metal. In a split second she was surrounded by a cacophony of screeching and grinding, then horrible human shrieks of shock and agony....

Terrified, she sat bolt upright as her car teetered precariously. An earthquake? In France? Impossible! She didn't know what to do! Dared she move? Would a slight movement tip her car over?

Then she saw bright red flares in the darkness, and soon a few men came running past her window shouting orders. Desperately she strained to make out what they were saying, but the moans and wailings that filled the night made it impossible.

Slowly, although askew, her car seemed to stop its rocking. They must have had an accident. What had happened? Gingerly Karen climbed up toward the door of her compartment and lowered the window. She was met with a blast of freezing air and a wall of driving snow. Ahead toward the train's engine she saw more flares and dark figures groping in the snow as people crawled or tumbled out of their compartments and emergency exits.

At first she couldn't quite make out what had occurred, but gradually her eyes adjusted to the darkness. About three cars behind the engine one car was virtually upended, and the next two or three cars were either off the tracks at a dangerous slant or had come uncoupled and were on their sides.

"My God," she whispered in disbelief and shock. Over the confusion and din she could hear people weeping—men as well as women—and anguished cries. Stuart's car was up there, too. . . . Had he been injured?

Carefully Karen pried open the door and looked down. It was a long drop, but the snow would break her fall. She quickly pulled on her boots, grabbed her coat and made the jump with her heart in her throat. Her only thought at that moment was to find Stuart, to be sure he was all right.

Once she hit the snow and stood up, she was knee-high and knew she wouldn't be able to stay out there very long. She had to keep moving! Heedless of the icy, soaked skirt around her legs, Karen waded through toward the engine. It was like a scene out of a war movie. Windows were shattered, and shards of glass reflected the redness of the flares. Suitcases, clothes and unidentifiable objects were scattered everywhere as if spewed from a volcano.

Confusion reigned, and the sobbing passengers who had managed to escape huddled over to one side. As Karen reached the car ahead of her own, she saw a young woman staring out of her door, frozen with fear as she clutched her baby to her bosom. A spiral of smoke had begun toward the end of the woman's car, and all Karen could think of was the possibility of a fire. "Jump!" she screamed at the woman.

Silent tears fell down the woman's face as she mutely shook her head. Her baby began to cry, but the young woman didn't seem to notice it.

"Jump!" Karen glanced around her to see if there was anyone who might help them, but the porters and conductor and engineer were busily trying to disengage the wounded and trapped.

Exasperated with the young mother's inability to move, frantic lest the train catch fire, Karen made one last effort. "Throw the baby to me," she screamed at her, holding up her arms. "Throw me the baby *now!*"

Though Karen couldn't hear her, she lip-read as the woman said over and over, "My baby, my baby . . . ."

"I'll catch the baby! He'll be safe! Then you can jump down!"

The smoke was getting thicker, and she could hear the Trans Europe Express employees shouting to everyone to stand clear of the train, to back away as far as possible. If there had been any question in Karen's mind before, their barked commands settled the matter. She tried again. "Do you want your baby to die? Listen to me! Throw the baby to me, then you will both be safe!"

As if in slow motion, the woman looked down at Karen with glazed eyes. A peaceful smile settled on her face as she lifted the child through the window.

As swiftly as she could, Karen moved under the spot so she would be sure to catch the infant—although even if she didn't Karen knew the snow would prevent any serious harm to the child. She raised her arms as high as she could, then watched as the mother closed her eyes and released her child.

Initially the child seemed suspended in midair, and then almost before she could brace herself, a blur of pink flesh and soft blanket rushed toward Karen, and she felt the jolt to her spine as she caught the baby. He had banged his forehead against her shoulder and was crying, but Karen strongly doubted that he was truly injured.

With the snow and howling wind whipping around her, Karen looked back up. "Okay! He's okay! Now it's your turn," she yelled. "The snow's deep enough.... *Jump!*"

Still wearing that serene smile, the woman turned away from Karen and disappeared inside her compartment. Panicking, Karen called out to her as she clutched the baby and held it against her breast with her coat wrapped around it. Seconds later the mother reappeared holding a makeup bag in her hands. She then put her shoulder to the door and half fell, half threw herself to the ground, just missing landing on top of Karen.

Incredulous, Karen could hardly contain herself. "You risked your life for your makeup?"

The young woman frowned. "Give me my baby," she demanded and grabbed the infant from Karen.

Before Karen could react, the mother turned and waded through the snow toward a group of passengers huddled near a stand of trees. Shaking her head, Karen could only believe that the woman was in shock and was not herself. *But*, she thought, *at least they're both alive.* And then she remembered Stuart.

Karen again forced her legs to plow into the snow, aware that the wind had shifted and was now driving against her face. To her left, just before what looked like a thick woods, she noted that a makeshift tent or lean-to had been set up, and that eerie green light sticks had been put into use. A number of men had set up a line to relay blankets from the train, and she could just discern two other men trying to build a fire for the gathered passengers.

"Miss," a man's voice said nearby and Karen turned. "Get over there with the others. You're just in the way here, and you'll get frostbite for sure."

"But I'm looking for my friend.... I've got to be sure he's all right," she protested.

The man gripped her arm firmly. "Lady, there are dead and injured in those cars ahead! The train's probably going to catch fire any second! Now hie yourself out of the way, y'hear? Get over with the others!"

She could see the furrowed scowl on his face and beads of perspiration despite the driving wind and icy cold. "But...."

"Do I have to carry you?" His voice was threatening, and he leaned toward her with clenched fists.

Karen took a step backward.

"Harry! Quick! Over here!" another man yelled from the torn wreckage of the second car.

Numbly she watched the man who had ordered her away break into an awkward trot. *Please don't let it be Stuart*, she prayed silently. And then the total horror of what was happening began to sink in. The scene swam in her vision. A strange whistling started in her ears, and she dizzily tried to focus her eyes as everything around her turned yellowish.

A strong arm was placed around Karen's shoulders. Leading her toward the group under the lean-to, the stranger scooped up a handful of snow and rubbed it across her forehead. "Stuart," she muttered feebly, looking up. But no, the man was the porter on her car.

"Come along, Miss Stockwell, you can't help anyone out here."

"Wh-what happened?" she managed to ask in a broken voice.

He shook his head sadly. "As best we can figure out right now, it must've been ice heave. The ground froze, snapping the rail's ties out of the ground. As the train passed over, the rail shot through the floor of the third car like a spike. Right now I think we have more injuries than dead people, but just about everyone's in a state of shock." The porter helped her to where the other passengers milled about listlessly and asked one of the men to keep an eye on her.

Most of them were in their nightclothes, shivering against the cold. A couple of men were busy trying to shovel away the snow from the ground, using parts of the wreckage to clear the area so their feet wouldn't freeze. At least she had her winter coat and boots. "Here, I can help," she said to one of them.

"Good," a gray-haired man said. "Grab anything you can and shovel quickly. A lot of these people will end up amputees if we don't hurry." Then he glanced over his shoulder and called to the men trying to get the fire started. "What's taking you so damned long? We'll all freeze to death!"

"All the branches and twigs are wet," one of them snarled impatiently. "We're doing the best we can!"

"Then get some paper and get it going! For pity's sake use money if you have to but build that fire!"

Karen had found part of a seat from the train and was using it to push away the heavy snow that had accumulated. All around her were the sounds of whimpering and babbling, of people groaning in pain. The exertion was keeping her warm, but trying to work with the heavy coat was cumbersome. She paused, took the coat off and then saw an elderly lady trembling with only a flannel nightgown to ward off the cold. Crossing over to her, she said, "Here, put this on. You can give it back to me later."

Tears came to the woman's dulled eyes. "Bless you, child."

"She's going!"

Karen looked toward the train, a sick horror creeping through her as she saw billowing black smoke pouring from the shattered windows and opened doors. Something like a loud hissing filled the night, followed by muffled explosions.

Everyone stopped what they were doing, all eyes glued to the wreckage. And then as if a fuse had been run the length of the train, the fire shot down the cars at incredible speed. Moments later there was nothing to see but twisted cars creaking between the intense heat inside and the bitter cold of the night. Like writhing bodies, they lurched and buckled in mechanical death throes as flames consumed the Trans Europe Express train.

The gray-haired man who seemed the leader of their particular group stood near her, openly weeping. "My wife's in there," he choked.

"But . . ." Karen could hardly believe her ears. Would he have abandoned her just to save his own life?

"She died instantly," he continued. "The impact broke her neck—there was nothing I could do."

Karen stared at him at first, letting the information sink in. Then she went over to him, easily making out his features in the illumination of the flame-engulfed train, and put her arms around his shaking shoulders. There was nothing she could say, she knew that. All she could do was offer what little comfort her body contact might give.

She was aware that slowly people were quietly resuming their tasks. Ironically the men managed to get a small bonfire lighted, although the warmth from the train's inferno could be felt even where they stood.

"Do you suppose anyone was trapped inside?" someone asked fearfully.

No one answered. No one wanted to think about it.

Then in the distance Karen heard the singsong whine of an emergency vehicle—maybe several of them. Help was on its way. For the dead nothing more could be done. For the living . . . it was a night none would forget.

Chapter 4

As the train continued to blaze against the blackness of the night, most of the people in Karen's group tried to get as close to the bonfire as they could, waiting for help to reach them.

"Does anyone know where we are?" the gray-haired man asked.

One of the porters who had joined them—a young man of no more than twenty—nodded. "Somewhere between Tournus and Mâcon. It's a long, curved stretch, and the Senozan forest is all along there," he said, pointing into the darkness beyond. "There's a highway paralleling the tracks," he added, explaining, "I come from a village quite near here."

"Do you suppose anyone saw what happened?" a woman inquired anxiously. "How far is the highway?"

"Not all that far," the porter replied. "But the real problem will be getting the emergency vehicles through the trees and the snow. Usually the highway's rather well traveled, but it's night and in this blizzard. . . ." he shrugged.

"Well, obviously *some*one got the word out," the gray-haired man said, "or we wouldn't be hearing those sirens."

"How do you know they're headed for us?" another man asked. "They could have had a call for a fire somewhere else."

"But surely," Karen put in, gesturing to the flames still engulfing the train, "someone can see *that!*"

"Right," another man said. "Whether those emergency vehicles were headed for us or not, any damned fool could see that blaze for miles. Help is on its way, no matter how they found out about it!"

The elderly woman who had been wearing Karen's coat tapped her on the arm. "Here, child, take your coat back before you freeze."

"No, no," Karen protested. "I'll get it later when we're rescued." Actually she felt parboiled in front and like an ice cube in back despite her frequent rotations trying to keep her entire body warm.

"My dear, listen to an old woman. I am eighty-five.... Do you think it really matters if I die tomorrow or next year? But you're young with your whole life ahead of you. Don't waste it trying to be noble."

Karen was shaking her head, marveling at the woman's willing self-sacrifice despite the fact that it could easily kill her. "I couldn't," she replied quietly.

"Here," the young porter interrupted. "I've got two blankets around me. I need only one, and we'll be rescued soon anyway."

"Snow seems to be letting up a little," a man remarked.

"No, it's just that the wind has shifted again."

And then they all fell silent. Perhaps fifty feet or so

away Karen could see similar groups of people huddling around bonfires, and she fervently hoped that Stuart would be among them. Her ears, despite their total numbness, picked up the sounds of the heavy equipment as it seemed to draw abreast of them somewhere in the darkness.

A loud, crunching noise filled the night, and they all turned in the direction of its source. Soon Karen saw flashlights bobbing and realized that men were coming toward them. As they lumbered through the drifts of snow, Karen saw that they were firemen.

"Hi, there!" The gray-haired man turned and waved at them as if their group couldn't be seen against the background of the burning train. "We've got some injured people here," he called out.

Karen noticed that many men were emerging from the woods, and the crunching mechanical sounds grew louder. Finally searchlights were visible, and she realized that the fire department had brought tractors to level a path through the trees. Behind them snowplows scraped a clearing so that the fire engines could get through.

Suddenly a great cheer went through the night as the passengers and employees of the Trans Europe Express realized that rescue was at hand. The first fireman to reach them held up his heavily gloved hand. "Okay, quiet down," he instructed firmly. "I'm Captain Bryant of the Tournus Fire Department. Who's in charge here?"

Everyone looked to the gray-haired man. "Unofficially I suppose I am. My name's Duprez, Felix Duprez."

"Good," Captain Bryant said. "I've got two ambulances on the main road, but they'd never get this far."

"Only two?" Karen was aghast. She knew perfectly

well that there were dozens of people seriously injured—the stillness of the night had carried their moans as clearly as a radio.

The captain glanced at her reprovingly. "More are on the way, miss. We put out an all-points bulletin instantly, even before we left the station. Every vehicle and all personnel we can muster have been called in," he answered. Then he turned to Felix Duprez. "We'll want the most seriously wounded first," he said. "My men are bringing litters, but if necessary, we can use blankets, too. I'm putting you in charge of this, Mr. Duprez. Go tell the others to get ready to help us load up the injured. All able-bodied men can help us carry them through the woods to the ambulances."

"Most of them have no shoes," Felix explained, gesturing to his own nightclothes.

"Do the best you can," the captain urged. "Even if your people can get the injured just up to the edge of the woods, that would leave my men free to take the litters from there."

Felix nodded. "I'll need some help in spreading the word," he said.

"Let me," Karen volunteered instantly.

"A man would probably be better for the task," Felix replied gently.

"Why? I have boots, I'm not injured . . . and besides, I'm looking for someone. We got separated after the wreck."

"Your husband?"

Thinking quickly, she answered, "My fiancé."

"Come along then," Felix agreed. "But remember, the main point is to get everyone organized so those who need medical attention receive it right away. Understood?"

"Clearly."

Reaching the other groups was infinitely easier now that the plows had cleared the way. "Some icy patches, miss, be careful," Felix called over his shoulder.

WITHIN A HALF HOUR every person knew what to do and was busy helping others to their feet or lifting passengers onto the few litters that were available. But even though Karen had gone to each cluster of huddling people, Stuart Macloud was not among them. With every passing minute Karen's heart grew heavier and heavier. She worked with the survivors with the sick conviction that Stuart had perished either in the wreck or in the subsequent fire.

She tried to put it out of her mind, realizing the greater urgency of saving passengers who had escaped. Karen reminded herself that she had only just met Stuart, that it wasn't as if he were truly her fiancé. But still...such a vibrant young man, so full of life! To die so senselessly....

At length, perhaps two hours later, all the injured had been removed from the site, and the rest were all in one place near the spot where the crews had initially broken through the woods. "All right," Captain Bryant said. "We have another problem."

They remained silent, shivering in the cold now that they were standing still. In the background the charred remains of the train steamed into the night as the fire engines pulled away. With engines running, they stopped alongside the passengers.

"Those of you who have the strength left," the captain went on, "will have to walk to the hunting lodge about a mile and a half from here."

"In our bare feet?" someone demanded incredulously.

The captain's face was impassive. "This isn't Paris, mister. This is farming land, and there are very few vehicles available. The local people probably slept right through the wreck—and even if they haven't, very few of them can afford a car. In a couple of hours it'll be dawn. Maybe then we can dispatch a few men to drive over to the farmhouses and get the residents to hitch up their carts."

"Wouldn't it be simpler just to telephone," a woman asked.

The captain smiled wanly. "These are poor people, ma'am. If they have to make a phone call, they go to the local pub or café."

"It would seem that we have little choice," Felix interjected levelly, fatigue etched on his features. "Either we wait here until morning, hoping to get rides on available carts—or we start walking."

A low moan of complaint went up, and Karen couldn't blame her companions. After what they'd all been through—the fear and shock, the blizzard, helping to remove those who couldn't walk—none of them had much strength left. For her own part all she wanted was a warm, dry place to lie down. A hot bath could wait! She glanced around at the faces of the others. "At least if we keep moving, we won't freeze," she suggested.

"That's right," someone else said. "Besides, what's to say it won't start to snow again—how would we find our way out of this place?"

A murmur of assent followed. "It's better than stand-

ing around here like the pampered, spoiled people we
really are," a woman's nasal voice piped.

"C'mon," Felix urged with a broad sweep of his arm.
"It's not a death march, but a life march! If this were a
war, you'd be shot for hanging back." He grabbed one
of the green light sticks, and some of the others did
likewise.

Grateful that she now had her coat back, Karen took
the first steps toward the path that had been cleared
by the tractors. Out of the corner of her eye she could
see the captain giving directions to Felix. Gradually
others fell in behind her.

Feebly, bodies aching, they filed into the woods away
from what was left of the Trans Europe Express. When
they reached the main road, they paused to get their
breath and reassemble. They watched as the fire equipment pulled onto the road and left them behind. Like
confused children abandoned in the middle of the wilds,
they followed Felix and Karen—although no one was
moving very quickly.

"I gather you didn't find your fiancé," Felix said to
Karen as they trudged along.

"No," she answered, a lump forming in her throat.

He patted her arm. "Don't despair, miss. The captain
told me that a couple of people were thrown clear of the
wreckage and have been taken to the hunting lodge
where we're going."

"Alive?" she asked, her hope renewed.

"He didn't say."

ABOUT A QUARTER OF A MILE from the hunting lodge a station wagon came toward them. It stopped alongside
Felix and Karen, the young driver leaning out the win-

dow. "Is this the whole bunch of you, or are there more?" he inquired urgently.

Felix shook his head wearily, huffing for breath. "No, some of them just couldn't take another step. You'll find a few about a half mile from here and a couple more closer to where the wreck occurred."

"Okay," the driver said with an air of the legionnaire. "I'll get them first, and if there's any room left, I'll stop for you on my way back." He grinned encouragement, rolled up his window and roared down the road.

Karen smiled wanly. "By then we should have reached the Senozan lodge."

Bedraggled, their small group resumed its march, and not too long afterward they could see the lodge nestled in the hills. The building was aglow with lights from the windows, which turned the snow before them a rich yellow. The sky beyond was only beginning to turn gray, and the ribbons of black predicted that the following day would be overcast at best, or there would be more snow at worst.

Finally they reached the parking area to one side, and half staggering, Felix and Karen were the first to enter the main lobby. A worried-looking matronly woman approached them.

"All the rooms are taken," she said apologetically, then helped Felix into an overstuffed armchair in the lobby. Karen didn't wait for an invitation but just sank into the nearest chair. Slowly the others struggled inside and took chairs wherever they could. "How many of you are there?" the woman asked, alarmed.

Karen could see that Felix's breathing was labored, and that he was terribly pale. "About fifteen, maybe twenty," she replied, certain she'd never move again.

The woman shook her head helplessly. "We were about half-full with paying guests before we heard about the accident," she said. "The ambulances took the seriously injured to the hospitals at Tournus and Mâcon but left the others here. We have no more room," she said adamantly.

"What about servants' quarters?" Karen asked.

"We've already used those that were available."

"Cottages," Felix mumbled, his chin against his chest. "Don't you have guest cottages?"

She nodded. "Two. But they sent over six nurses who are sharing them. They're very small," she added.

"I'll settle for the floor," Karen said, and a few others echoed her sentiments. "At least it's dry and it's warm. All we need are blankets—dry blankets. Right?" She looked at the other survivors who nodded mutely.

"But our guests! We can't have wall-to-wall beds!"

"My God, woman—don't you realize that this is an emergency? If your 'guests' had any guts at all, they'd give up their beds!"

The woman stared at Felix, absorbing his outburst with apprehension. She was spared any comment by the appearance of a nurse.

"I'll take over here, Mrs. Montague," she said briskly. "I'm the head nurse assigned to the lodge," she declared to the group in a firm, no-nonsense tone. "Nurse Clarissa Nantoux, of the Tournus Hospital." As she introduced herself, the nurse walked among them to see just how badly off they might be. "Mrs. Montague, remove the cushions from the chairs and couches and arrange them on the floor—not too close to the fireplace. Some of these people are suffering from severe frostbite."

As if they could finally afford to display their emotions, some of the passengers from the train began to weep openly. "Is there any coffee?" Karen asked. "Anything warm?"

Nurse Nantoux turned to the hotel manager like a general glaring at a corporal. "Well, Mrs. Montague? If there's some broth, that would be better than coffee."

"The cook hasn't come on duty yet," the manager replied ungraciously.

"Then I've just appointed you the cook. Surely you know how to make broth!" Seeing the disgruntled woman shuffling off, she turned to Karen. "You seem a little stronger than the others.... Help me spread the cushions on the floor."

If Karen hadn't been so exhausted, she might have laughed. Did the entire world believe she possessed superhuman strength? Yet with extreme willpower Karen managed to stand up. She swayed for a moment and looked over at the nurse silently. The woman nodded to her, urging her forward. Feeling as if nails had been driven through all her joints, Karen leaned on chairs and end tables, and began to pull the cushions to the floor.

In the meantime the nurse was carefully removing the draperies from all the windows, helping the others to lie down and covering them carefully. "We're short of blankets," she explained. "All right," she said to Karen, "it's your turn. As a reward you can stretch out on the couch.... Even without cushions it's more comfortable than the floor."

Gratefully Karen sank onto the padded springs and felt the last of her strength seep out of her. She fervently hoped she wouldn't have to move again for at least three

days. Dozing, almost in a stupor, Karen was later aware
of the head nurse lifting her by the shoulders, holding a
cup of hot soup to her cracked lips. Karen sipped at it,
glad of its soothing warmth, hoping it would restore
some of her strength.

"Can you hold the cup by yourself," the nurse asked
gently.

"I—I think so."

"Good. I'll help the others."

"What time is it?" Karen asked feebly.

"About five. It'll be at least another hour before daylight filters through—not that I expect it to disturb the
sleep of anyone in this room."

"Is everyone safe?" Karen wanted to know, still only
half-awake.

"Yes, the others were brought in about a half hour
ago. Drink your broth now. You've done more than
anyone could have expected of you."

Karen snorted silently. It was too close to what Franz
Kleimer might have said to her. Foggily she watched the
nurse attend to the others, taking them the steaming
mugs and cups, and offering sympathy. She was only
dimly aware of another nurse moving between the
cushions on the floor, performing similar tasks. But
soon, even before she could finish her soup, Karen put
the cup down and fell back on the couch asleep before
she knew it.

In the course of the dawn hours her dreams brought
back the dreadful scene she had witnessed, and as much
as she wanted to turn over, to put the images out of her
dreams, she was too weak to accomplish it. At one
point she even dreamed that Stuart Macloud was kneel-
ing beside her, stroking her face. But of course, that was

impossible. If he had survived at all, Stuart would have been taken to hospital; he'd not been among those left behind to make that final hike. And then mercifully she fell into a deep undisturbed sleep. . . .

DULL DAYLIGHT MET HER FLUTTERING LASHES as Karen roused from sleep. It took her a few seconds to realize where she was and why. The cup of cold soup still sat where she had put it, and she tried to reach it. Every fiber of her being ached at the attempt, and she gave it up. Lying there, she listened to the exhausted snores that filled the lobby of the lodge, and she wondered what would happen next. Would they be able to stay there for a few days, regaining their strength? Or would that miserly, uncaring woman throw them out? Karen didn't know.

Someone moaned in his sleep, and she sympathized with him. But it was over. . . the worst was definitely over, and they would all go back to their regular lives soon, trying to forget what had happened on the Trans Europe Express. Again she drifted off to sleep, occasionally aware of the nurses checking to be certain they were all right. At one point she thought she heard a man and woman whispering over toward the doors that seemed to lead to a dining room, but she didn't care. Maybe it was a guest wondering where all these people had come from, complaining about his ruined holiday because of "them." It was more than she could cope with. . . . She was too feeble to feel any kind of guilt about it. It wasn't her fault anyhow. Had it been up to her, she would already be at the hotel in Nice, dreading the afternoon's auction. Well, that was one worry she no longer had. . . . If the mask of Lugalki was a fake, it wouldn't be Franz's money that was wasted.

Later she became aware of someone shaking her gently. "Miss? Miss?"

"Wh-what?" Her blue eyes opened and beheld Nurse Nantoux.

"Here," the woman said, seating herself on the edge of the couch. "I've made some nice hot oatmeal with honey. That should make you feel better. Come along now, you need it."

"I . . . I just want to sleep," Karen mumbled.

"You can," the nurse said firmly, "after you've eaten something. We're waking all of you now, but you can go back to sleep after you've had some nourishment." The woman was holding a spoon to Karen's lips with a squinting command in her eyes.

Carefully Karen raised herself on one elbow and glanced around. There were two other nurses present and a couple of people Karen assumed worked at the lodge. They were rousing the others, bringing bowls of cereal from trays. She came fully awake then and gingerly propped herself up against the arm of the sofa. "I can do it," she said to the nurse, taking the bowl and spoon. "The others probably need you more."

"Feeling better?" Nurse Nantoux placed a warm hand on her forehead, then took her pulse.

"Like I'd been hit by a Sherman tank. But I can sit up, thank you. What time is it?"

"About one o'clock. The lodge's guests are in the dining room, but we've screened all of you off so you wouldn't be disturbed or embarrassed. The lot of you are the talk of the hotel," she added with a little smile.

Karen guessed her to be a woman in her early forties, a little stout but in a motherly sort of way. Her dark brown hair was sprinkled with gray, and she wore no makeup at all. "I guess we've kept you up all night," Karen said.

The woman patted her arm. "We're used to it. We're constantly on call day or night. Besides," she added, "none of us had to go through the trauma the rest of you did."

Karen tried to smile but failed. "Thank you, nurse."

"Oh, just call me Clarissa. I despise formality except in situations of duress. People respond to commands better if they feel intimidated." She stood up and, crossing over to one of the trays, took a bowl to a passenger who was just waking up.

Karen watched them as they hand-fed the others, grateful for their concern and efficiency. At first she hadn't been aware of her hunger, but after a few spoonfuls of the bracing cereal she realized she was famished. The honey was especially good, totally unlike the kind bought in stores. It was thick, almost granular, and lent a nutty taste to the oatmeal.

She glanced over to see how Felix was doing. Although some of his color had returned, she was worried about him. Then his eyes caught hers, and he smiled his good morning to her. She bobbed her head gently, trying to convey that she was glad he was all right. Then she looked around the room at the others, relieved to see that all of them seemed to be able to sit up and eat.

Whatever their politics, their careers, their attitudes toward life or other people, all of them now shared a common bond. They had experienced something rare together, something that might have killed all of them...and they had survived. How could it affect the rest of their lives, Karen wondered. Would they face their own mortality, reaching out to get as much from life as possible? Or would the return to routine, the pressures and frustrations, reestablish old patterns? It was an interesting speculation, and Karen almost wished they could somehow keep in touch. She laughed mirthlessly. For what? The annual reunion of the survivors of the Trans Europe Express? To do what? Repeat every year how glad they were to have come through?

Trying to shake off her thoughts, Karen carefully moved her legs, then eased them over the edge of the couch. She caught Clarissa's eye and beckoned to her. "Is there any way I could take a bath?" she asked when the nurse reached her.

"Can you walk?"

"I think so." Actually she wasn't that sure.

"All right. Use my cabin. I'm sharing it with two other nurses but they're both on duty now. The door's open, so just walk in. You'll find clean towels in the cupboard next to the sink."

Already anticipating the opportunity to be clean and wash her hair, Karen hesitated, a slight frown on her face.

"Use my comb and brush," Clarissa said, reading her thoughts. "They're in my overnight bag along with my makeup."

Karen glanced up. "But you don't use any."

"There hasn't been a chance since I got here," Clarissa laughed. "The shades will probably be wrong for your coloring, but it's better than looking like a peeled onion."

Smiling at the image, Karen pulled herself unsteadily to her feet, then made her way between the others on the floor toward the front door of the lodge. She paused at the doorway and looked back at Carissa.

"It's the cottage on the right," she called.

On shaky legs Karen let the brisk winter air revitalize her as she walked slowly toward the small cabin. Once inside she noted that two of the beds had been slept in, but a rollaway bed still stood folded by one wall. At its feet was an overnight case with the initials CN embossed in gold on its side. She smiled, then went into the bathroom, turned on the faucets and began to disrobe.

A half hour later, although she had put on the same clothes again, she was at least clean. It had taken her more than five minutes to comb the snarls out of her shoulder-length hair, glistening clean at last. Checking the makeup kit, she saw that Clarissa had several shades of lipstick and selected the one that would go best with her fair complexion. Fleetingly she wondered what had happened to that young mother and her infant, but she realized that they were probably all right. Perhaps they were among the lucky ones to get rooms at the lodge.

Feeling infinitely better Karen let herself out of the cottage and walked back to the lodge. Curious, she decided to use a side entrance beyond a large veranda that was probably used only in the summer. There were two sets of double doors leading to the inside, the panes of glass sparkling even in the dullness of the day.

Along one low wall potted plants waited grayly for the spring to bring them back to life. On the other side wooden benches lined the wall, presumably so guests could enjoy summer breezes. Actually it seemed a very comfortable and pleasant place, and except for the ungracious Mrs. Montague she wouldn't mind coming back to spend her holiday here. Oh, not right away, but someday. And then it suddenly occurred to her that Franz Kleimer thought she was in Nice...probably bidding on the mask right then. *I've got to find a telephone*, she realized.

Would Franz have heard about the train crash on the news? Were he and Ilse worried sick that she might have died? And what about the Ferriers! They'd be sick with worry if the news media had already picked up the story.

She'd simply have to telephone both places collect. Obviously her handbag had gone up in flames with the train. Karen only hoped that she could get through at least to Franz or Ilse. Even if Maria and George weren't at home, Ilse would keep trying to get through to let them know that Karen was all right.

Quickening her pace as much as she could under the circumstances, Karen opened one of the doors, then stopped dead in her tracks.

There, seated at a table in the dining room, was Stuart Macloud. . .and a dark, exotic-looking woman was with him.

"Stuart," Karen barely breathed, her eyes filling with tears.

Chapter 5

She stood nearly transfixed as she observed him, ignoring the woman for the moment. Stuart's head was bandaged, and there was a piece of tape over his left eyebrow. Otherwise, judging by his liberal gestures, he seemed to be all right.

Then she took in his companion. Dark, probably from Latin America, she sat directly across from Stuart, her shoulders hunched tensely as if to ward off a blow. But even from the doorway Karen could see that the woman was a beauty, probably with a great deal of Indian blood: high cheekbones, sparkling obsidian eyes and a small aquiline nose over provocative scarlet lips.

Whatever it was they were talking about, it was obviously not a pleasant subject. They seemed to be arguing, although their voices were not raised. She seemed to be trying to convince Stuart of something, and he was apparently adamant in his refusal or rejection.

Suddenly as if sensing that he was being watched, Stuart looked up and saw Karen. With a happy grin he swiftly got to his feet and came toward her. "Karen! I didn't think you'd be awake for hours yet."

"You knew I was here?" she asked, too delighted to see him to question how he'd gotten to the lodge.

His hazel eyes seemed half-amused, half-worried. "I heard the hotel's station wagon when it returned and came downstairs to see if you were among the passengers. I had been sick with fear that you'd died in the crash. Then when I saw you asleep on that couch, I wanted to hold you close, to tell you that everything would be all right."

She felt slightly faint, as if finding him had been too much of a shock—even though a grateful one—for her on the heels of what she'd been through. "Did...did you touch my face?"

"Why, yes, I did," Stuart replied. "Then the nurse came over and insisted I leave you alone. She practically dragged me away. I'm afraid I told her a lie," he said, gazing down at Karen steadily. "I told her I was your fiancé so she'd let me stay with you."

Karen had to smile, recalling that she'd used the same ruse. "But...I looked for you everywhere," she said, confused. "If you weren't taken to the hospital, how did you get to the lodge?"

"Here," he interrupted, pulling out a chair for her. "You're looking rather pale."

"Stuart," the woman called to him with a pronounced accent. "Shall we finish our discussion before you chase after a new 'conquest'?" Her sarcasm was unmistakable.

He waved her question aside. "Later, Adela. Besides, I think I've made my position quite clear," he added with an edge to his baritone voice.

Glowering, the woman rose, pushed back her chair

and flounced out of the dining room. It wasn't prudence that prevented Karen from asking what that was all about...but the greater curiosity and concern about Stuart's presence at the lodge. "Will you please tell me how you got here?" she repeated, thankful for the chair he'd provided. Apparently she hadn't regained as much strength as she had supposed.

"I must have been thrown from my compartment at the time of impact," he said, seating himself across from her and looking into her blue eyes intently. "I don't know how it happened frankly. I don't even remember feeling anything at all. One moment I was lighting a cigarette, thinking about how I could arrange to meet you in Paris as quickly as possible—and the next thing I knew, I was being rushed to the hospital for X rays."

"Your head...." Karen's hand went toward his face with concern, then she pulled it back, frightened of hurting him.

"Only a concussion. A couple of bruises and cuts. The doctor said they'd probably remove the bandage tomorrow or the next day—that it's merely precautionary."

"Thank God," she whispered. "When I couldn't find you, I was almost certain you'd died. You were in the car that was ripped open by the rail, and I thought...I thought...."

The corners of his full mouth turned down in a derogatory smile. "Shhh, don't upset yourself," he soothed. "I'm invincible—surely you realized that between the martini and the liqueur."

"This is no time for levity, Stuart. I've been scared out of my wits that you'd perished...and after what we've both been through, let's not make light of just how vulnerable we all are!"

"Everyone has to die at one time or another," he said indifferently.

"My God, Stuart! How can you say such a thing? Those who perished had lives to lead...families. Don't you care?"

"You're cross with me," he said, feigning hurt.

She sighed heavily. "No, not really. And I suppose it's different for me than it was for you. You didn't hear the suffering, see the wounded or watch the train go up in flames. You didn't witness all those people in their nightclothes, half-frozen in four feet of snow till help came."

Stuart bowed his head for a moment, and when he looked up at her again, his expression was serious. "I'm sorry," he said. "You're right. I didn't really 'experience' anything—not like the rest of you anyway. I shouldn't make jokes about it. Were there many fatalities?" he asked soberly.

Karen shook her head. "I haven't heard anything by way of statistics, but I overheard that at least thirty people died."

He drew his thick eyebrows together. "Poor devils—what a way to die!'

"We can only hope it was instantaneous," Karen said, trying to obliterate the moment when the train became a holocaust, and someone had asked if anyone had been trapped inside. It was one thing to have your neck broken and never know what had happened...and quite another to be pinned inside an inferno, burning to death. Karen shuddered, not wanting to think about it and upset by Stuart's cavalier attitude. Although he had agreed with her a moment before, Karen felt sure that he had done so simply to appease her, not because he was genuinely concerned.

How different he seems, she thought. Last night he'd been amusing, yes...but only at his own expense or about some of the lunacies of life. At no time had Stuart seemed indifferent to the problems of others. Yet today he appeared to be almost apathetic...though he had concealed it right away. Could it be, she wondered, that a concussion could cause a temporary personality change? She supposed it was possible, but she knew so very little about such things.

"...And it gives us a wonderful opportunity to get to know each other better," Stuart was saying.

"Wh-what?"

"I said that life must go on," he repeated, a rather rueful expression on his face. "Regardless of how awful last night was, at least we're together again."

She stared at him, shocked by the shallowness of his remark, then tried to convince herself that Stuart simply wasn't himself. "I...I have to make a couple of calls to Paris, Stuart. Let people know I'm all right. If you'll excuse me," she said, rising with difficulty.

Getting to his feet instantly, he steadied her. "Can you make it alone?"

"Yes," she replied simply, still bothered by Stuart's change in attitude. Slowly she made her way back to the lobby and found the front desk. Mrs. Montague wasn't on duty; instead, the young man she'd seen in the station wagon was tending it.

"Yes, miss? May I help you?"

Briefly she explained that she had to make two calls to

Paris but would call collect. To her relief he agreed immediately.

"Just about any of you who can walk have asked to use the hotel's telephone. Of course, you'd want to notify your husband and relatives that you're all right." He came around from behind the desk. "I've got to mind the switchboard," he said, "but you can use Mrs. Montague's private office. It's just two doors down."

"Mrs. Montague?" Karen questioned apprehensively.

"Oh, it's all right," he reassured her. "She's gone to her quarters for some rest. I know she comes across as an unfeeling, greedy person, but she's not so bad once you get to know her. Don't forget," he urged sympathetically, "that if the owners of the hotel get a lot of complaints about the inconvenience to the paying guests, it could cost her her job."

"I suppose you're right," Karen conceded. "I hadn't looked at it from her point of view."

The young man grinned. "Just don't stay on the line too long, please. Others will want the same privilege as the day goes on."

"I understand," Karen replied, then made her way down the wood-paneled hall of the lodge to a door marked Private. Just in case, she rapped lightly, but getting no response, she opened the door gently. Inside was a medium-sized room. One wall was lined with old, scratched filing cabinets, and its facing wall had built-in bookshelves housing boxed files and ledgers dating back to 1809. *How peculiar*, she thought, amused, *to keep records that can't possibly be of any use today*. On the other hand, she reasoned, that was the stuff from which history was reconstructed.

She went around to the heavy, carved mahogany

desk where a vintage telephone squatted. Lifting the receiver, she heard the desk clerk say, "Just a moment and I'll give you an outside line," then the dial tone. Karen only hoped that if Mrs. Montague found out that he was letting them use her private line, she wouldn't fire him. Then she dialed the operator, giving her the Ferriers' number first.

When the phone rang seven times without being answered, she tried the gallery. Jenny's cheerful voice answered, "Kleimer Gallery, good afternoon." She accepted the collect call readily. "Hi! How's Nice?" the young woman asked merrily.

Karen couldn't assume from her question that the news of the accident hadn't been broadcast; Jenny never listened to the news and turned off the TV the moment it came on. "It's too depressing," she had always said with an aura of inability to do anything about the world's problems.

"I'm not in Nice," Karen answered finally. "Is Franz or Ilse in?"

"They both are," Jenny responded, curiosity and surprise evident in her tone. "Whom do you prefer?"

Karen decided that Ilse would take the shock better than the infirm Franz. A second later Ilse Kleimer came on the line. "*Oui?*"

"Ilse, this is Karen."

There was a brief pause. "Oh, my dear child," Ilse whispered with a choke in her voice. "We, Franz and I, feared the worst when we heard the news this morning. Then, not hearing any word from you, or any list of survivors...."

Karen could hear the relief and gratitude in the older woman's voice as she called over to Franz that Karen had lived through the wreck. He couldn't have been too far from the telephone because she heard his outrush of breath as he exclaimed, *"Merci de Dieu!"*

"Where are you, dear?" Ilse asked, getting back to her.

"I'm not exactly sure," she answered with a light laugh. "Some hunting lodge between Tournus and Mâcon in the Senozan forest."

"Let me speak to her," Franz said in the background.

"In a moment, darling," Ilse said to him. "But are you all right," she asked, her mouth again turned into the receiver.

"Exhausted, but no broken bones. I was one of the lucky ones." She was touched by the tone of genuine concern and warmth in Ilse's voice. While Karen had always liked the woman, even admired her, she had never been certain how Ilse had felt about her other than as a reliable employee. It was nice to know she really cared about her as a person. "Look, Ilse, I can't tie up the line for long. I wanted you both to know I was all right and to ask you to call my foster parents for me. I tried to reach them earlier, but they weren't in. If they hear the news, I'm worried George might have a heart attack."

"Of course, my dear . . . what's the number?"

Swiftly Karen gave her their names and the telephone number, thanking Ilse for her aid. All the while she could hear Franz clucking irritably, wanting a chance to speak to her. Laughing, Ilse finally turned the phone over to him.

"Karen, are you all right?"

"Yes, Franz. I can't stay on the line, but Ilse will tell

you. I'm really sorry about not reaching Nice, Franz. I suppose the mask of Lugalki was snapped up...."

He *tsk*ed with ironic amusement. "You needn't worry about it, my dear." His tone was almost gleeful. "It was stolen!"

"What?" She could hardly believe her ears...much less that the old man could be so delighted about it.

"Yes, yes! Cagliani telephoned this morning around nine, wondering if I knew precisely where you were. He was trying to make a case out of your not showing up to pinpoint you as the thief." He chuckled, then began to wheeze.

Karen didn't know how to react. She supposed it *would* seem suspicious that the mask was gone, and one of the invited bidders hadn't shown up. Cagliani had no way of knowing what mode of transportation she had used to reach Nice.... For all he knew, she might have flown down, then spent the night in a hotel as a base of operations...then like a one-woman S.W.A.T. team had somehow absconded with the mask. That her integrity was questioned irked her, yes; but under other circumstances she might have found it less upsetting.

"What I don't understand, Franz," she said, "is why you seem so glad about the theft."

"I don't really expect you to," he answered a bit more seriously. "It's rather like a jilted lover, I suppose. If I can't have the mask, I'm delighted that no one else can, either!"

"The thief has it," Karen reasoned logically.

"Yes, yes, but he'll try to sell it. He has to at some point—and maybe by then the gallery will have made a few sizable sales so I can afford to pay more for it."

She shook her head, perplexed by his convoluted

thinking. "Eric thinks it's a forgery, Franz. It was in his report to you yesterday morning." She heard her own words and marveled that she could think in terms of days and hours after all that had happened in between.

"I know he does," Franz replied. "But I'm sure he's wrong this time."

"How can you be so certain?"

"Art dealers have their ways, Karen." Then he returned to his earlier thoughts. "Thieves cannot risk taking stolen goods to museums, but they know there are a few unscrupulous dealers who will ignore the law if the price is right."

"You've been contacted?" she inquired, shocked.

"Not as such. Everyone knows I would never buy stolen goods no matter how priceless. But I'll hear about it, mark my words."

"And then?"

He laughed dryly. "Then we'll see, Karen. We'll see. The main thing is that it wasn't purchased this morning, which means it's still on the market—one way or another."

"I suppose Cagliani was disappointed to learn I'd been on the Trans Europe Express," she said, still not quite understanding Franz's attitude.

"He hadn't even heard what had happened when I spoke with him. But he did let slip that Ian Macloud had sent his son to bid on it, and I was delighted to know that old reprobate wasn't going to get his hands on it!"

"Macloud," she mouthed into the receiver.

"Yes, the multibillionaire shipping tycoon. He has a storehouse of treasures that rivals what J. Paul Getty amassed—except that Ian Macloud hides everything from the world. He's a jealous lover of art, my dear, and shares his hoarded treasures with no one! That's truly criminal!"

Still taken aback by the information, Karen asked, "Do you know him?"

"We've run across one another over the years before my arthritis crippled me. Why?"

"Because," she replied slowly, "I met his son on the train. We had dinner together, and he knew perfectly well I was on my way to that auction. He didn't say a word to me about being on the same mission."

"Perhaps because he's cut from the same cloth as his father—a cagey old buzzard if ever there was one."

Perplexed, even a little hurt, Karen explained to Franz that she had telephoned collect and was not surprised when he suggested they hang up right away. She promised she would call again as soon as she knew when she'd be returning to Paris but asked that he wire her some money for her fare. He reluctantly said he would, then said goodbye.

Karen remained seated at the desk, deep in thought. Why hadn't Stuart told her that he, too, was going to bid on the mask? Had he merely been trying to draw her out, find out how much she was authorized to bid for it? Or had he known all along who she was, perhaps arranging for their accidental meeting at dinner? Was that why he had seemed so charming last evening and strangely distant and different today? Since neither of them had reached Nice...had his purpose, his interest in her, proven needless?

And yet it wasn't that he hadn't shown concern for her today. Or for that matter during the dawn hours as she slept. No, there was something else...his seeming disinterest in the ordeal of the survivors. How could anyone be callous about what had happened? Oh, he'd covered his feelings quickly enough when she had gently upbraided him, but still. . . .

Then much against her wishes a nasty and suspicious thought crept into her mind. Anyone could put a bandage around his head and a strip of tape over one eye! Who was to say that Stuart had really been injured at all? Wasn't it possible that in the panic and chaos he had made it to the main road and hitched a ride to Mâcon? From there rented a car and driven straight to Nice in the dead of night? He could have stolen the mask, then returned. . . with a perfect alibi for where he'd been.

No, she thought, her mind recoiling at such a prospect. Yet wasn't it possible? Wouldn't it be a coup for Stuart's father if he could steal the mask instead of pay for it. . . or worse, be outbid?

Much as she hated herself for having such thoughts, they certainly weren't beyond the realm of brilliant strategy. There was only one way that she could think of right then to dispel her theory. She would have to go to Tournus and check the hospital records! Had he specified which hospital they'd taken him to? No, not that she could remember. Well, then she would simply have to check them all both in Tournus and Mâcon.

And if there was no record of Stuart being treated? Karen closed her eyes tightly, fervently hoping he had told her the truth. She didn't want to believe that Stuart was capable of such a thing!

Chapter 6

Much of the balance of the afternoon was spent trying to help get things organized at the lodge. Clarissa Nantoux, looking haggard with dark circles under her eyes, was still tending the wounded upstairs and popping downstairs to the lobby to check in from time to time.

Finally around half past three Karen had pleaded with her to go to her cabin for some much needed rest. "You'll be useless to us if you collapse," she had urged.

"You're right, of course," Clarissa admitted. "There are five other nurses, after all."

"And I'm feeling much stronger. Why don't you let me take a poll of who's up to moving to some other inn so we don't make things more difficult for everyone. None of our group is seriously hurt. . . . We're just worn out."

Clarissa's lips set firmly in a determined line. "Don't think of removing any of the patients with frostbite," she ordered. "The doctors will be coming over this afternoon to examine the patients upstairs and in the lobby.

Some of the patients upstairs will probably be well enough to move elsewhere so we can give the frostbite victims their beds until we've more room at the local hospitals."

Karen had to smile. No matter how hard she worked, or how much sleep the woman had lost, she was a professional through and through. "All right, Clarissa," she agreed. "Now you just leave everything to us and get some rest."

After shooing the nurse out of the lodge, Karen took a deep breath and looked around her. All but maybe five or six in her group seemed infinitely improved. And if some of those on the second floor of the lodge were sufficiently better to be discharged from medical care, that would ease the hotel's burden considerably—at least clear the lobby of its refugees.

Felix Duprez had dozed off and on most of the day but seemed much better now. She crossed over to where he sat and asked if he needed anything.

"Do you realize, I don't even know your name," he commented wryly.

She smiled, sharing the humor. "Stockwell, Karen Stockwell. Do you feel up to making a few phone calls?"

His glance was openly questioning.

"Many of us could move to inns and get out of the way here. Though what we'll use for money, I don't know."

"Don't worry about that," Felix remarked sagely. "All our expenses will be picked up by the railroad, rest assured. But you'll find a paucity of inns in this area," he added.

"How do you know that?"

He chuckled. "I'm with the Department of Tourism. But certainly it's worth a try."

"Felix...." She wanted to tell him how sorry she was about his wife's death but didn't quite know how to begin.

Obviously he intuited what she had wanted to say by the tone of her voice and her sympathetic expression. "Please, let me pretend—for just a while at least—that we're merely separated. I know I'll have to deal with reality once I'm back in Paris—but not now. Can you understand?"

"I think so," Karen replied softly, wondering how she would react under the same circumstances. Even when she had believed Stuart to be dead, hadn't she busied herself by trying to help the others? *Yes*, she admitted to herself, *but he's not my husband. My situation can't be compared to Felix's!* And then she realized that she hadn't seen Stuart since their meeting in the dining room...and for the first time she wondered who the woman was she'd seen him with. It was plain that they knew each other very well; strangers didn't argue. Besides she had called him by name. Was he avoiding her, sensing her disappointment in him? Or had he gone to his room to rest...because of his "concussion." *If he has one*, she reminded herself.

She watched Felix make his way over to the desk. It wasn't so much that he was limping as it was that she could tell every bone in his body ached; his walk was almost disjointed, uncoordinated...which she could certainly understand. He borrowed a small telephone directory from the young man at the desk, then ambled down the hall toward the manager's office.

The sound of a car pulling up in front of the lodge

caught her attention, and Karen walked to the front
door to see who it was. The hotel's station wagon came
to a halt, and she was surprised to see Mrs. Montague
climb out from behind the wheel with an ox of a man
getting out of the passenger side. The back of the wagon
was filled with something, but Karen couldn't make
out what it was. She only hoped that Mrs. Montague
wouldn't head straight for her office and find Felix
there. But then if he told her he was with the Department of Tourism, Karen was confident the manager
would see the merit of cooperating with him. After all,
Felix would be in a position to do her a great deal of
good . . . or quite the reverse.

To her surprise the matronly manager was actually
smiling as she came through the door, followed by the
huge man. She clapped her hands twice, calling for attention. "I've good news," she proclaimed loudly as if
the lobby were an amphitheater without microphones.
"Jacques and I have gone to the local farmers and explained your problem. We've gathered clothes from
them and their wives! Mind you, they'll have to be
returned—they're poor people and need their meager
belongings. But they have understood your plight and
are willing to do what they can."

Well, I'll be, Karen thought. She really wasn't such a
bad sort after all! Man's humanity to man had always
affected Karen far more than his inhumanity, and tears
welled in her eyes as she observed the handshakes and
thanks the announcement had triggered. Jacques then
went outside and began to lug in the assorted rough
clothing, spreading garments everywhere so people
could try them on in hopes of an approximate fit. The
first-class passengers of the Trans Europe Express might

have sneered at such peasant garb under other circumstances, but they were openly appreciative right then—delighted to have something to wear besides pajamas and robes and nightgowns. A renowned couturier couldn't have received more approbation than these humble garments evoked.

Just then Felix crossed the rustic lobby and stood next to her. "I may have compromised the department," he said with a self-deprecating laugh, "but I've firmed up six rooms—doubles—and have coerced the owners of the inns to put cots in the dining rooms when they've been vacated after supper."

He paused, only then perceiving what was taking place. "Are there any shoes?" he asked Karen eagerly.

"Boots," she responded. "Some slippers, too, which will probably be a better fit for the women."

Felix nodded his head appreciatively. "I may never again go to bed unless fully dressed. Excuse me, Karen, but I want to see if there's a size forty jacket in that collection—and a pair of trousers that will span this paunch!"

As if the heavens were watching over them...the clouds began to disperse, and the sun was coming out. It would be dark by four or five, but at least it gave them all some cheer and hope.

AT SIX O'CLOCK just as some of the first passengers were being transferred to other inns—five at a time in the station wagon—Karen set out to find Stuart to tell him she was leaving the lodge. Mrs. Montague was once again behind the desk, and she asked for his room number.

The woman threw her hands up in the air impatiently. "How would I know? In the middle of the night these

casualties were sent over from the hospitals! There was
no time to register anyone! I don't even know who *you*
are!"

"A young, handsome man with his head bandaged,"
Karen urged. Then she gestured to her left eye. "And a
piece of tape. About six feet tall, brown hair . . . ?"

The corners of the manager's mouth turned down as
she narrowed her eyes trying to recollect such a person.
"There was a fellow," she began. "I remember him only
because he came in hours after the others . . . almost as if
he were all alone."

"Did he have an angular face . . . more like a Scotsman
than a Frenchman?"

"Poof! They all looked alike at that hour," the
woman exclaimed impatiently. "But you can check for
yourself. I put him in room 208. Go up and see for yourself if he's the man you mean." With that she turned her
back on Karen and plugged a line into the hole beneath
the flashing light on the switchboard.

Karen dreaded climbing the uncarpeted stairs; the
exertion of the afternoon was catching up with her. Still
she couldn't just leave the lodge without saying goodbye. Besides, if her suspicions about Stuart were accurate, she wanted to be sure she didn't lose track of
him. Then, too, if she was way off base, and Stuart was
totally innocent, she certainly didn't want him to
believe she had no interest in him at all!

With set determination Karen took hold of the
banister and mounted the stairs cautiously. Finally, a
little out of breath, she reached the second floor. Since
the staircase was on the extreme left of the upstairs, she
didn't have to decide what direction to take. The second
floor was even more rustic than downstairs, with the

heads of deer mounted along the broad hallway. The walls seemed to be made from mortar or rough plaster, and exposed beams crossed at strange angles. The doors to the rooms were of unhewn planks, and wrought-iron handles served as the only relief.

Since it was already pitch black outside, the electric lights had been turned on, casting eerie shadows as she slowly walked down the hall. Finally she reached room 208 and knocked lightly.

No one answered.

She tried again a little more loudly and waited. No response. It was possible, of course, that he was asleep, but Karen strongly doubted that. Other than the bandage on his head Stuart had appeared to be in fine condition earlier. It was far more likely that he simply wasn't in his room. With that in mind she tried the handle and, finding it unlocked, opened the door carefully. "Stuart?"

Silence.

Karen didn't know what she should do. While it was unthinkably rude to enter someone's room without permission, certainly the unusual circumstance warranted a bit of leeway. Feeling like an intruder, Karen nonetheless entered the room.

He wasn't there. *Now what do I do*, she asked herself. She decided that since she'd come this far she might as well leave a note. She turned to the small writing desk beneath the dormer window and opened the middle drawer, where she found the expected hotel stationery and postcards along with a couple of ballpoint pens. Taking a sheet of paper, she hesitated for a moment. What if this wasn't Stuart's room? She rested the tip of the pen against the blotter, then wrote:

Please note: This message is intended for Stuart
Macloud. If I have the wrong room, perhaps you
would be kind enough to give it to him.

Stuart—I stopped by to let you know that we're
being moved to other inns in the area. I don't know
which one I'll be at, but I'll try to call you tomorrow and let you know.

Karen stopped, the pen poised, wanting to add something that wouldn't make it seem as if she had been chasing after him—something that might appeal to his sense
of humor:

Certainly hope they remove the bandage tomorrow. You look like an albino sheikh!

Best, Karen

Then she placed the note inside the frame of the mirror
above the dresser so it would be easily seen.

Her eyes fell on the half-open top drawer,
and she noticed two packs of cigarettes and car
keys. The cigarettes weren't the brand he had been
smoking the evening before, but then perhaps the
lodge didn't offer many choices. The car keys, however, bothered her. Were they his own? He, too,
had been fully dressed at the time of the accident....
Would a man take his car keys with him on a trip?
Wouldn't he leave them at home? And if so, where
had these come from...other than a car rental
agency?

There was no personal distinction about the key ring;
no initials, much less the Cartier sort of thing she would
have expected him to carry. Just an aluminum ring with

two keys to a Renault. Surely Stuart didn't drive such an inexpensive car in England!

What had Mrs. Montague said earlier? That she remembered this man because he had seemed to arrive all alone? Couldn't Stuart have awakened the owner of the nearest car rental agency and driven himself up to the lodge...bandaging his own head before entering the lobby?

She was tempted to open the drawer to see what else might be inside, but her upbringing simply wouldn't permit such an invasion of someone else's privacy. She didn't even approve of the police searching people's property...though she knew they had to do it if they were to apprehend criminals. "But I'm not the police," she whispered to herself almost regretfully.

It was important to her to know what she should believe about Stuart. Had she been more attracted to him than she had realized? And then she recalled her observation about how similar Stuart was to Alex and knew that part of her desire to confirm or dispel her thoughts was because of that. She didn't dare risk falling in love with another charlatan.

Swallowing hard, Karen began to back away when some movement reflected in the mirror caught her eye.

"What are you doing here?"

Behind her, just inside the door, was the woman Karen had seen with Stuart earlier. Her coal black eyes were blazing with open hostility and spite.

"I...I...."

"You are spying," the woman hissed, her soft accent turning harsh.

"I'm doing no such thing," Karen retorted hotly. "As you can clearly see for yourself, I've merely left Stuart a note!" She pointed to the mirror, and while she realized she should feel smugly righteous, she felt awkwardly guilty instead.

"Let me explain something to you, Miss Stockwell," the dark woman said with controlled venom.

"How do you know my name?"

The woman smirked coldy. "Stuart told me," she replied. "But you listen to me. Stay away from him! Stuart has nothing to give you. . . . He is mine! Now get out of here," she snarled, crossing the room and ripping the note out of the mirror.

Indignant, yet knowing she had no business to be in Stuart's room, Karen walked out the door with as much dignity as she could muster.

But in the hallway she heard the distinct sounds of her note being torn to shreds. . . and a triumphant laughter deep in her adversary's throat.

Now Stuart would never know that she had tried to say goodbye. . . .

Chapter 7

The transfer to the other inns had been smooth, and after a hearty, but simple, supper most of them had gone straight to bed. Karen had waited for a little while, rather hoping that Stuart would be trying to locate her. He'd certainly have no difficulty seeing that the lobby had been vacated, and if he was really interested in her, surely he'd go to the trouble of calling the few inns in the area.

But by nine o'clock when she hadn't been paged, Karen decided that he wasn't going to call. Perhaps that Adela woman hadn't left him alone for a moment; perhaps he didn't care where she was anyhow. The mask of Lugalki had been stolen...and his interest in her had ceased. Surely that was clear, even if it did hurt her feelings. At least, she thought, the degree of his interest had been defined before she had gotten to know him better...or worse, fallen in love with him.

She had gone upstairs, undressed and climbed under the soft eiderdown cover with mixed emotions. Much as

she didn't want to think that Stuart Macloud was a conniving, unscrupulous sort, his behavior that morning—
coupled with the feasibility of his having stolen the
mask—left her little choice. For that reason Karen particularly wanted to get a good night's rest. She wanted
to rent a car in the morning and check out hospital
records in the vicinity. Karen was sure it would be
wisest to appear in person, sensing the staff would be
more inclined to give her the information than if she
merely telephoned. Franz had wired her enough money
to do this, and she wasn't worried about not having a
driver's license anymore. She was confident that any
rental place would believe it had been lost in the train
crash.

But the more she thought about Stuart as a possible thief, the more her logic rebelled against the idea.
How could he have possibly known that the train would
have an accident? Even if he had rigged it himself—silly
as that idea seemed—would he have risked his own life
just to swipe a mask his father could easily afford?
It would be entirely too stupid, and even if she had
misjudged him initially, Karen knew Stuart was not a
fool.

Yet one way or another Karen planned to return to
Paris the next day. If she could find no record of treatment at any hospital, she would have no alternative.
She would have to tell Franz, who in turn would report
it to the authorities. However, if there was a record, she
would know that his behavior had to be connected with
his injury and hope that someday he would telephone
her. *Well*, she thought as she lay in bed, *it takes less
energy to be positive than to be negative!* And with that
nebulously comforting thought she fell asleep.

In the morning Karen awoke feeling almost like her usual self. Some of her muscles were still a little stiff and sore, but she was one hundred percent improved. Through the window of her room she could see that it was a gloriously beautiful day. Huge billowy clouds lumbered across an ice blue sky, and the snow crystals sparkled like sequins. She was glad to note that the roads had been plowed; it would make her task just that much quicker and easier.

Bathing quickly, she put on the underwear she had washed out the night before and then her dress. Unfortunately it was one of those imitation suede fabrics, and there was no way she could rinse it out. Karen made a mental note to stop at a drugstore and buy some makeup...and if she saw a modest boutique, maybe she'd even buy a different dress or a sweater and skirt. She was beginning to feel as if she had lived in her clothes, and she couldn't wait to put on something else.

An hour later after a hearty country breakfast and a quick stop at a nearby drugstore, Karen had at least put on some makeup and was arranging by telephone to rent a car. The local garage handled such things, and they apologized for having so few cars available; apparently many of the train's passengers had also rented cars with the intention of driving home. "We're a small town, miss," the man said. "We have very little call for rentals as a rule."

Suddenly an idea popped into Karen's head. "Tell me," she opened casually, "did you happen to rent a Renault to anyone the night before last...late at night?"

"Just a second, I'll check."

When he came back on the line, there was a tone of surprise in his voice. "Why, yes, as a matter of fact. My

partner was on duty—though he'd been sound asleep.
A woman arranged for the rental, saying she'd been on
the train and had to return to Paris immediately."

"A woman?"

"Yes, here it is. Miss Iris Calderón. She filled out the
application as a citizen of Argentina."

Karen let the matter drop, not wanting to arouse any
suspicion. She was positive that Iris Calderón was the
same person Stuart called Adela. How many Spanish
accents were there in Tournus? And how many people
would want to rent a car in the middle of the night?
Had Stuart put her up to it though? Or had it been
Adela's idea...and for that matter why hadn't she
returned to Paris?

Since the car keys were in Stuart's possession, Karen
was fairly confident that Adela had rented the vehicle
on his behalf. Did that mean that there were two of
them involved in the theft of the mask? Was that the
basis of the argument between them that Karen had
witnessed? It did indeed, now that she thought about
it, have the intensity of a thieves' falling out.

Her rental arrangements made, Karen determined
that she would find out as much as she could before
she also returned to Paris. If those two had the mask,
then it had to be right in Tournus with them. The
sooner she acted, the greater the chances of its
recovery...before either of them tried to get away.

She waited in the lobby, her thoughts in turmoil,
for the car to be brought around to her. Karen had
already made a list of all the nearby hospitals and
had received instructions how to get to them from the
concierge. There were two in Tournus, a small
emergency facility about twelve miles south on the N.6
route, which paralleled the Saône River. It was an-

other seventeen or eighteen miles to Mâcon, where the concierge told her that there were at least three hospitals.

Much as she dreaded having to drive south only to have to drive back again when she headed for Paris, she had no choice. At least the distances weren't vast. It wasn't as if she had to drive to Toulouse and back! Since Mrs. Montague had said that the seriously injured had been divided among the hospitals in the two towns, she had to check them all out—including the facility between them.

SHE WAS BACK AT THE INN by two o'clock, bitterly disappointed. No Stuart Macloud had been admitted by any hospital. Karen even described him, thinking he might have given an assumed name, but she was assured that no one by that description had been treated. Moreover, bandaging a concussion was an archaic practice; they had practically laughed at the idea.

Now she knew. No ands, ifs or buts. While she had no conclusive proof that Stuart had actually driven to Nice and stolen the mask...why else would he bother with the pretense of being injured? He was extremely clever, there was no doubt about that. Given the opportunity to pull off a crime and get away with it scot-free, Stuart had grabbed his chance and succeeded.

The greatest irony, of course, was that Karen herself would be his strongest alibi. If put on the stand and questioned, she would have to testify that she had had dinner with him that evening...and that, yes, he had been at the lodge along with the others. Even the most elaborate premeditated crime couldn't compare with how easily Stuart had pulled off the theft of the mask of

Lugalki. Who could possibly suspect him? *I do*, she conceded sadly.

She checked out of the inn, torn between feeling depressed and feeling glad that she hadn't become more involved with Stuart before learning the truth about him. Getting behind the wheel of the rented car, she knew she had better get back to Paris right away. There was nothing more she could do in Tournus except worry or feel sorry for herself, and it was at least a three-and-a-half-hour drive to the city limits. She'd get back to the Kleimer Gallery at nearly closing time.

Karen eased the car into gear and began her journey back, unable to appreciate the scenery. During the whole trip she kept turning the matter over and over in her head. Her only "evidence" that Stuart had stolen the mask was circumstantial. Two things plagued her: one, why he had lied about his having a concussion; and two, the difference in his personality when they met in the hotel dining room.

It didn't particularly surprise Karen that Stuart had pretended to be traveling alone. If he had wanted to pick her brains about how much Franz Kleimer was willing to bid for the mask, it was only smart to keep Adela out of sight. Yet, how had he *known* that she would be on that particular train? She could have taken an earlier one or driven down to Nice. Unlike an airline reservation there was no formal record of her passage on the Trans Europe Express. So had he been merely lucky? Had Stuart taken a guess and been right?

It seemed pretty farfetched, yet how else could she account for the coincidence? And, too, she was still bothered about his motive for stealing what his father could afford. The game? The risk? Karen supposed it was possible. She had no idea of how rich people's minds worked.

But by the time she got back to Paris, Karen could no longer think straight. She had been through entirely too much, and there were too many contradictions for her to sort through. She would put it all before Franz and let him deal with it.

There was a light, cold drizzle as Karen parked the car on the Rue du Faubourg St. Honoré, then crossed the street to the gallery. As had happened upon her return from Oslo, Karen felt as if she'd been gone weeks instead of a couple of days. Most of the snow had melted, and what was left was a sludge, brown and grimy from exhaust fumes and soot. When she pushed open the glass doors this time, however, Karen felt somehow older. The notion of "turning in" Stuart weighed heavily on her, but she knew it had to be done.

This time she had no suitcase to tuck behind a desk, no purse. She had decided earlier against wasting time by shopping for a different dress to wear. Karen walked into the Kleimer Gallery wearing the same clothes that she had left in and went straight upstairs. The door was ajar, and after rapping lightly, she walked right in. Ilse was seated with her legs curled under her, going over the week's receipts; Franz was at his desk, head bowed over a pile of forms from Mr. Lund's gallery in Oslo.

She gazed at them for a second. A frozen tableau of life going on as usual. Would her own world ever be the same again, Karen wondered. But at that moment Ilse's head came up, and with a little cry of delight she came over and hugged Karen.

They all exchanged greetings, and it didn't escape

Karen's attention that Franz had had to dab at his eyes a couple of times.

"Have you any idea of how lucky you are to be alive?" Ilse demanded as they seated themselves. "More than one hundred and fifty-eight people were killed, and there are sixty-two others still on the critical lists."

Karen bowed her head, swallowing hard. "No," she replied, "I had no information about just how many fatalities there were."

"They showed the wreckage on the news last night," Franz commented softly. "It's a miracle anyone survived at all."

"But you're safe and you're home," Ilse chirped, trying to lighten the atmosphere. "I reached your foster parents about an hour after your call yesterday. Fortunately neither of them had heard about the crash. They were vastly relieved to know you were safe, Karen. They obviously love you very, very much."

Karen smiled. While she knew the Ferriers loved her, it was good to hear it nonetheless. "Have you had any further word about the mask of Lugalki?" she asked Franz. Hoping against hope, Karen desperately wanted to hear that it had been returned, or that the criminal had been apprehended.

He shook his head, a playful smile on his lips. "I spoke with Cagliani this afternoon, and he was still trying to pin the crime on you. I told him he might as well try to accuse Sir Ian Macloud's son—that stopped him!"

"You may be closer to the truth than you realize," Karen replied slowly.

Franz leaned forward in his wheelchair, his dark eyes taking on a concentrated expression. "What do you mean, my child?"

As calmly as she could, Karen revealed what she suspected. She explained the distances involved, how Stuart would have had plenty of time to get to Nice and return...and her check of the various hospitals. Karen didn't fail to mention the sultry Adela, either. If she was his accomplice, the police should know about her, too.

At the end of her report Franz took a deep breath and sat back in his chair. "That's quite a tale, Karen."

"But why should this young man want to steal it?" Ilse asked, a perplexed expression on her handsome face.

"I don't know," Karen answered candidly. "I've tried and tried to think of what reason he might have...but I keep coming up blank. Unless, that is, you want to consider the challenge of such a crime as sufficient motive."

Franz scratched his gray head, then drew his forefinger across the base of his thick mustache. "It's conceivable. I've read about such things from time to time. The idle rich, bored, seeking adventure—it wouldn't be the first time. But at such a moment, thrown from the train, in four feet of snow—when would a sane person have the time to come up with such a scheme?"

Karen gazed at him, her blue eyes widening. "Maybe he isn't sane," she said under her breath. "It might account for his change in personality the next day."

The old man began to drum his fingers on the arm of his chair. "Yes, I can see that Ian Macloud might stoop to such a thing. Perhaps the theft had been planned in advance, carefully worked out. That would make more sense than a spur of the moment decision to rush off to Nice—especially under the circumstances."

"But if that were the case," Karen interjected, "then why didn't Stuart simply have dinner with Adela and be

done with it? He didn't have to go to the trouble of
singling me out."

Franz smiled kindly. "You were already tired when
you boarded the train, Karen—then to go through that
terrible accident had to be added pressure. What makes
you so sure he was deliberately trying to get information from you? Perhaps his companion, Adela, wasn't
hungry. It didn't have to be a conspiracy or a plot. To
that extent I would accept mere coincidence." He turned
to his wife. "Wouldn't you, Ilse?"

"I'm not so certain," she replied calmly. "There are
times when logic interferes with reality.... At times
intuition is a better judge."

"Bah! You and your woman's intuition," Franz said in
mock anger.

Ilse shook her head. "Everyone has intuition, Franz, if
they are receptive enough to listen." She turned and
looked at Karen. "You're confident that Stuart Macloud
seemed different the next day?"

"Yes, quite."

"What about his injury?" Franz interrupted.

Karen glanced at him. "What injury? It was all a lie."

"Yes, but if he was attempting to fake one, perhaps he
used a change in attitude to support his ruse."

The three of them fell silent for a few moments, turning the information over in their minds. Finally Ilse
broke the stillness. "No, Franz, I believe we should rely
on Karen's feelings. I think you're right that this young
man and his father had previously planned the theft...
and the train accident merely provided a perfect alibi,
even as Karen said. As for arranging to have dinner
with her alone, I don't know if that's true or not. Actually it doesn't seem to matter very much does it? The

mask is gone. Sir Ian Macloud wanted it, and sent his son to be sure he got it."

Franz Kleimer nodded his agreement. "No risk of being outbid, and being the sort of man he is, Macloud would never have to worry about anyone seeing the mask in his possession."

"What about his wife, Lady Macloud?" Karen asked. "Surely she would have heard about the theft and put two and two together."

"Possibly not," he responded. "I've heard that Macloud has devoted an entire wing of his mansion to his collection of art. Maybe she's not permitted in there—or perhaps she has no interest in such things. Macloud could have the mask until he died, and no one would be the wiser."

"And you can't send a dead man to prison," Ilse commented.

"Except that it wasn't the father who stole it but the son. He would still be very much alive."

Franz shook his head. "Proving his guilt would be nearly impossible, Karen. He was on that train with you, seen by all those people and then again at the lodge. What's to prevent him from denying any knowledge of how his father came to have the mask?" The old man frowned, creating deep furrows on his brow. "My sorrow, Karen, is that I shall never see the mask in my lietime—much less own it."

She looked at his stooped shoulders, and a rush of compassion filled her. "The police?"

His gnarled hand lifted and eloquently denied her question. "And tell them what? That it was physically possible for young Macloud to get to Nice and back? It was equally possible for anyone on that train, Karen, as long as they weren't severely injured. You could've done it, too. So could the conductor or your chum from the Department of Tourism!"

"But most of us could be accounted for the entire time. We were either stranded together in the snow or being watched over by nurses! Stuart arrived at the lodge hours after the first arrivals, yet ahead of my group. Every one of us can prove exactly where we were!"

"Franz, she has a very good point."

Sighing, the old man straightened in his chair. "Even if the police thought we had a case," he said slowly, "do you want me to file a complaint against the son of one of the richest men in the entire world? Why, Macloud would eat me up and spit me out! He'd sue me for libel and take everything we've worked so hard to create, Ilse! It isn't as if we had any real proof. Can you imagine the district attorney being pitted against the best legal minds money can buy? He'd be laughed out of court, and our world would be destroyed."

Franz wheeled over to where his wife sat and patted her hand gently. "No, darling. There's nothing we can do."

"But all your hopes and dreams for the mask . . ." she pleaded.

"I've got an idea," Karen offered.

Franz looked up at her. "And that is?"

"My foster father, George Ferrier," she said eagerly, the thought taking form. "He's a retired police detective. George would know how to gather the evidence we need . . . and he has access to information that we don't. A few discreet inquiries . . . ."

Her employer began to smile, his dark eyes taking on a look of hope. "Do you think he'd do it?"

"There's no harm in asking," Karen answered.

"We would be happy to pay him for his efforts," Ilse said.

Franz's expression clouded only momentarily. "Yes, of course, we'd pay him," he concurred somewhat gruffly.

"But, dear," Ilse said, a probing look in her eyes, "are you absolutely certain you want this young man to be proved guilty?"

Karen returned her glance levelly. "If he is, he should be punished. If he isn't, well, then my seeing Stuart again is up to him. But at least I would know that he's innocent." Karen pushed a strand of her tawny blond hair away from her eyes, hoping Ilse couldn't tell how very much she wanted to believe Stuart wasn't guilty.

"Then you must speak to your foster father as soon as possible," Franz said emphatically.

"Tomorrow," Karen said, rising. "Right now all I want is a—"

". . . Hot bath and a good night's sleep," the Kleimers said in unison and they all laughed.

Chapter 8

Sunday morning Karen telephoned her foster parents and asked if she might drop by a little later in the day.... There was some advice she needed from George. Maria had explained that he'd be watching the soccer matches on TV, so to come by after four. Her foster mother also thanked Karen yet again for having telephoned them the moment she was back in her apartment the night before; while they knew she was all right, both of them felt far better knowing she was at home.

She hung up, still appreciative that the apartment manager had extra keys. Otherwise, she would have had to bother her foster parents and spend the night with them. After all that had happened, she wanted to be in her own place.

Karen fixed herself an appetizing breakfast, wondering what to do with the time between then and four o'clock. Naturally her thoughts kept straying back to Stuart Macloud, how charming and handsome he was. . .and then his almost flippant attitude the day after the accident. Perhaps even more important her ego had been bruised by Stuart's failure to attempt to find her. Karen wasn't a vain person, nor did she have an aggrandized version of herself. But he had seemed so sincere when he'd said good-night to her, saying he wanted to see her again. It hadn't been one of those cliché "We'll-have-to-get-together-someday" remarks; he had meant it.

Reflexively her hand went to the cheek he had kissed before he had gone on to his own compartment two cars ahead. Then Karen remembered something. Hadn't Stuart made some mention during dinner of having an apartment in Paris? A nicely appointed place so he didn't have to stay in hotels whenever he was in town? Yes, she was sure of it. But where? As rich as he was, he could doubtlessly afford a luxury suite on the Boulevard Suchet across from the Bois de Boulogne. But that hadn't been it.

Karen tried to remember. She recalled that she had been somewhat surprised by the neighborhood he lived in. While it was certainly a very nice one, more than she could possibly afford, still it wasn't in the area she imagined a wealthy young man would pick. *Perhaps*, she thought, *he has to live on his salary. That would explain it.*

She knew there was a park on his block—he'd said something about how nice it was to look out his living-room window and see the trees in the various seasons. But where? "Why do I care," she asked herself aloud, faintly bitter.

Yet she knew the answer to that. She was downright curious about Stuart, how he lived, what tastes he had.

Then, too, she rationalized, were he to return to Paris right away, Stuart would doubtlessly have the mask in his possession. If she could contact him, talk to him sensibly, maybe she could convince him to give it back. No one would have to know who had taken it.... He would have had his fun, but the priceless relic could then be restored to its rightful owner. Would Stuart listen to her? Karen didn't know. But she believed it was worth a try at least.

She pulled out the telephone directory just in case he might be listed. To her surprise he was: *Stuart Macloud, 8 Avenue de Messine: 555 34 84.* Of course! He lived on the Parc Monceau, she remembered that now. It wasn't too far a walk from her own apartment.

Since it was a bright day, Karen decided to take a little stroll over there and dressed casually in a good pair of winter boots, beige wool slacks and a black turtleneck sweater. With her camel-hair polo coat she should be warm enough. Then after brushing her tawny hair, she pulled out a shoulder bag that matched her boots and threw in the extra set of keys, a pack of tissues, her spare makeup kit and the change purse in which she kept her grocery money.

She was outside in the sunshine a few moments later, heading toward the Place de Clichy; she strolled leisurely on the Boulevard des Batignolles, west to the Place Goubaux. Even for a Sunday the traffic circle was congested, and Karen had a difficult time getting across. She assumed that most of the people were out for a drive on the first bright Sunday there had been in quite some weeks—despite the horrendous cost of gasoline.

On the other side of Place Goubaux the street became the Boulevard de Courcelles, and it was a short walk from there to the Avenue de Messine. She turned south on it, enjoying the park that surrounded the street. Karen had no idea of what she would do when she reached number eight, but that didn't bother her. Since she knew Adela had torn up her note to Stuart in Tournus, perhaps she would leave him another one. *And then he'll think I'm chasing after him*, she thought and concluded that it might not be such a wise idea.

When she reached his building, she was very impressed. A massive structure, though only three stories high, it had obviously been erected at least one hundred years before but had recently been renovated with modern improvements. The glass doors of the residence glided open for her automatically as she stepped on the all-weather carpeting outside. The entrance hall was spacious, bordering on luxurious, with a rich slate blue broadloom and paneling of rich, gleaming walnut. Off to the left was a private bar for the residents and their guests, but it was dark at that hour of the morning. On her right was a desk where a receptionist sat with a modern switchboard nearby. Behind her were small closed-circuit video screens panning every hallway in the structure as a security system. Just beyond, about three feet away, was an open arch that revealed a parcel room. A few chairs and sofas upholstered in dark red velvet were scattered around the lobby.

"Yes, miss, may I help you?" the receptionist asked politely.

Karen smiled. "Perhaps," she responded as casually as she could. "I was on the Trans Europe Express with Mr. Macloud, and I was just wondering if he got back safely."

The woman's face took on an alarmed expression.

"Wasn't it horrible!" She shuddered as if it had been her own experience. "And I'm so glad you stopped by," she said. "None of us knew if Mr. Macloud had survived the accident or not! Naturally we knew he was en route to Nice, but they still haven't published a list of survivors. Thank you for letting me know," the receptionist said appreciatively.

"Then he hasn't returned yet?"

"No. His keys are still here. It's a house rule at the Residence Parc Monceau that all tenants turn in their keys before leaving the building. That way no one can lose them only to be found by a professional burglar."

Karen's eyebrows rose. "That would drive me mad," she replied candidly. "I'd have no privacy at all!"

The receptionist shrugged. "Perhaps not, but it aids us in maintaining security. We haven't had a burglary in this building in three years, ever since we instituted the regulation."

The mere thought of having to check in and out was abhorrent to Karen—like schoolchildren having to get the key to the toilet from their teachers in front of the entire class. "What's to prevent them from having duplicate keys made?" she asked curiously. "It's the first thing I'd do if I lived here." Then Karen smiled, hoping to take the edge off her words.

Obviously the receptionist hadn't taken offense. "You'd first have to get past the desk without turning in your keys. All the locks were changed three years ago, you see."

"I suppose you're right," Karen conceded, yet privately she speculated on just how difficult it would really be. If nothing else, a tenant could make a wax impression and simply take it to a competent locksmith. "Well, anyway, I had only wanted to see if Mr. Macloud was back. He was very kind to me, and I wanted to thank him."

The receptionist nodded. "Would you like to leave him a note? I can give you a pencil and paper," she offered.

With such encouragement to do what she had wanted to in the first place, Karen couldn't resist. She moved to one side of the desk behind the telephone so the young woman couldn't see what she was writing:

Sorry to have missed you. Left a note on your mirror in Tournus. I'm back in Paris, so stopped by to see how your injury is. Hope you're a lot better.

Karen Stockwell

Folding the paper neatly, she handed it to the receptionist. "I gather he's in and out a great deal," Karen prompted, trying to seem merely friendly.

"Oh, perhaps six or seven days out of the month at most. His permanent home is in England...but I guess you know that."

"Of course," Karen answered, smiling warmly. She didn't know how long this receptionist had had her job, but she was far too open with strangers. "Doesn't give him much time to do any entertaining, does it?" she remarked idly.

The woman laughed lightly. "The only time I've ever seen anyone come to visit him—other than you, today—was last week. Some Latin type," she said, lowering her eyelids in imitation.

"Why, you must mean Adela," Karen said as if they'd been the best of friends. "Yes, she can be very standoffish when she wants." *And that's the understatement of the year*, Karen thought. "I daresay she came by to pick him up. She, too, was on her way to Nice."

"You don't think they're engaged or anything, do you?" The girl seemed disappointed.

"Well, if they are, they're keeping it to themselves. You said Adela came by on Thursday?"

"Did I? Let's see. No, it was Tuesday. She was draped in chinchilla and gold from head to foot . . . well, not her feet, but you now what I mean. To top it off, she arrived in a chauffeur-driven white Rolls-Royce!"

"Oh, that's just one of Adela's little affectations," Karen said airily but wondered where the woman had come by enough money to live so lavishly. Of course, such things could be had if one were willing to bend one's morals. . . .

"Well, I just hope Mr. Macloud isn't planning to marry her. I'd hate to see him tied down to someone like that. Oh, I'm so sorry . . . I forgot she's a friend of yours, too."

"That's all right," Karen said magnanimously.

"It's just that he's so straightforward and friendly. He always has a joke to tell us, and he's very generous at Christmastime. Mr. Macloud's just about everyone's favorite tenant!"

"I can certainly understand why, though he's always struck me as a little moody."

"Him? Not at all! He couldn't be a steadier, friendlier guy!"

"Well, thanks again," Karen said, turning away.

"He'll be glad to know you came by," the receptionist called cheerfully.

As Karen stepped back outside, she marveled that the

receptionist hadn't been fired years ago. In a position of that sort, discretion was paramount . . . yet the girl had been happy to disclose just about anything.

WHEN KAREN ARRIVED at the Ferriers, George had just turned off the TV set and was stretching. As she let herself in with the key they insisted she keep, he enveloped her in a bear hug. "No bruises, no broken bones?"

She smiled. "Nary a one," she replied.

"Maria," George called toward the kitchen. "Karen's home."

It had always given her a very warm feeling whenever they said that. To them their little home in St. Ouen would always be hers, too. Sometimes, of course, if she was feeling fiercely independent and rebellious, she had to bite her tongue not to remind them that she had her own apartment . . . her own life to lead. But those occasions were rare. Most of the time she was very glad to know that she could always come to them whenever she wished, and that they wanted her to be happy.

"Can you stay for supper?" Maria asked as she came out of the kitchen, wiping her hands on an apron. She approached Karen and kissed her lightly on the cheek, then she, too, looked her up and down to be sure Karen hadn't been injured.

"I'd love to if you've enough to feed me," Karen answered.

Maria smiled broadly. "Another potato, a few extra vegetables . . . these things are easily stretched, dear. Now tell us all about the wreck," she said, seating herself on the worn floral couch across from Karen.

"How about a little sherry," George said. "We've

much to be thankful for, Karen. You could have been killed!"

"All right," she said laughing. "But just one. Promise?" She knew all too well that George enjoyed his little nips before dinner. And while she had never known him to get drunk, Karen wanted him to have his full mental faculties when she asked his advice.

Briefly, yet she hoped dramatically, she told her foster parents about meeting Stuart—Maria all but fainted when she found out who his father was—and the accident that ensued. Karen minimized the unpleasant aspects so they wouldn't be unduly upset, emphasizing instead the bravery of her traveling companions. "And so," she said, winding up, "I rented a car yesterday and came home."

Maria shook her head gravely as she sipped at her sherry. "You make it sound so trivial," she complained.

Karen laughed. "Did you want all the gory details as some of the tabloids print?"

"No, of course not," George responded firmly. He tucked his thumbs behind his suspenders, stretching them outward. "Now, Maria said you wanted to consult with me about something."

"I'll go see about supper," Maria said, getting up.

Karen watched the older woman leave the room. It wasn't that Maria couldn't hear what she wanted to discuss with George, she just felt that Maria would worry needlessly if she knew too much. If George later wanted to tell her about it, that was fine with Karen. She took a deep breath and then told George about the mask of Lugalki and her theory about Stuart Macloud. When she had finished, she looked at George earnestly.

"Could you help us, George? Mr. Kleimer is willing to pay you for your services."

He slapped his hands on both knees and hunched his shoulders. "This is a very serious accusation," he said slowly. "I can see why your boss doesn't want to go off half-cocked."

"But do you agree that it's a logical assumption? Am I too imaginative, or—"

"No, no. Your reasoning is sound," he interrupted. "It's just that there's no concrete evidence, no proof. This will have to be handled very carefully and off the record, Karen."

She beamed. "Does that mean you'll look into it?"

"Oh, I'll make a few inquiries at the precinct tomorrow. While Nice isn't in our territory, the theft of something so valuable has to have been recorded in Paris. After all whoever stole it will have to sell it privately."

Karen nodded. "As you know, George, all such thefts are reported in a monthly bulletin that goes to every art dealer and museum in the world. Even if it's a fake, as our advisor believes, it's still made of solid gold and would be worth a fortune just melted down."

"How much does it weigh?" George asked.

"Two pounds."

"At the price of gold per troy ounce a smart crook might just resort to melting it down to avoid going to jail for stealing the mask. Yes, you may have a point there. I'll see if the department also can get the word to our snitches to be on the lookout for someone trying to sell gold."

"What about Scotland Yard?" Karen asked. "Stuart is a British subject after all. Should they be notified?"

"Dinner's on the table," Maria called from the dining room.

George got to his feet stiffly, extending a helping hand to Karen. "No, not yet. Let me first see what I can find out through my friends at the department. This Adela you mentioned—why do you suppose she used the name Iris Calderón when she rented the car?"

"For all I know," Karen said truthfully, linking her arm through his, "that may be her real name, and Adela is an alias . . . or maybe it's her middle name, and she just prefers it."

"I'll run a check on her. From Argentina, you said?"

"According to the garage."

When they were seated at the table, steaming dishes before them, Maria glanced across at Karen with an innocent expression on her face. "Tell me, dear, this Stuart Macloud. Is he a nice young man?"

Karen swallowed a smile. "Yes, very."

"And you say the two of you had a good time together?" Her plump hands lifted a bowl and handed it to George as she indicated to Karen to start with another.

"It was one of the best evenings I've had since Alex and I broke up," she answered honestly. However, she knew perfectly well that Maria was anxious for her to find a suitable husband and raise a family.

"That rat," George muttered vindictively under his breath, serving himself a generous portion of the savory lamb stew.

"I don't suppose," Maria said nonchalantly, "that he asked you for your phone number?"

"Maria, you're as transparent as glass!" George passed the stew to Karen. "You must stop playing matchmaker at every opportunity—Karen will stop coming home if you don't!"

"Karen smiled broadly, her blue eyes twinkling. "Never," she said, then turned to her foster mother. "He knows I work at the gallery, Maria. If he wants to find me, it won't be difficult."

Maria nodded smugly, shooting a triumphant glance at her husband. "Well, he would certainly be able to provide nicely for a wife," she stated archly.

George and Karen exchanged glances, but neither said anything. In her heart Karen wanted only to find out the truth about Stuart. Should she forget him entirely...or pray that he would telephone her soon? If he were a thief, she would have to put him totally out of her mind. But if George could prove otherwise, then she could hope to see him again.

Something on her face must have betrayed her thoughts. George leaned toward her, a question in his brown eyes. "Do I see what I think I do?"

Karen blushed with embarrassment.

"You're taken with this fellow—after only a couple of meetings?"

"Taken," she admitted slowly, still flushed, "but not in love."

"Nonsense," Maria chimed. "It takes only one look to know when you're in love!"

"After Alex," Karen responded with spirit, "I'd prefer to take a longer view."

"Very wise, Karen. I'm glad to hear you say that," George remarked, ladling out boiled potatoes sprinkled with parsley. "The world is far more complicated than it was when Maria and I met. Things happen too quickly, life is too uncertain. If love is real, it will last through more than two meetings."

While his tone had been fatherly, Karen understood the underlying message: Don't get too involved until we find out more about this man!

She was all too happy to go along with that philosophy.... She just didn't want it to take too long to find out!

Chapter 9

Monday was a day Karen would have liked to forget. The entire day was spent notifying creditors that her charge cards had burned with the Trans Europe Express and asking them to issue new ones. Then she had to go over to the Department of Motor Vehicles and apply for a replacement driver's license.

Fortunately with her recent promotion she had also been given a modest raise in salary. So it didn't hurt quite as much as it would have to buy another handbag, new makeup, have new keys to her apartment made and buy the several other items she considered necessary. A new briefcase could wait till later, as could a new suitcase and the items the old one had contained.

She was also keeping in mind what Felix Duprez had told her. "Make up a list of everything you lost in the fire and the replacement value—not what it cost you originally, but what it will cost you now," he had said. "Then submit it to the claims department of the Trans Europe Express. Their insurance will reimburse you,

Karen. There's no reason for you or any of us to have this accident dig into our pockets. We've gone through enough already."

Since she had been traveling light, it didn't take too long to prepare her list, and enclosing with it a brief letter, Karen had it in the mail by midafternoon.

Naturally throughout the day she kept wondering if Stuart had returned to Paris yet; or what George had been able to find out at police headquarters. It seemed—though she knew it wasn't really true—as though her entire world was hanging in abeyance. Looking at her life with utter candor, what did she have besides her job? Yes, one day it could prove to be a real career...but at present it was still just a job.

Meeting Stuart had been one of the brightest highlights of her life since she and Alex had broken up. She had dated a few times but had come back to her apartment wishing she had washed her hair or mended a few things instead. When would men learn that taking a woman out to dinner did *not* constitute a favor or a compromise?

Karen was weary of going out with men simply because they had asked her. But most of her friends were now married, and while they were still in touch, Karen sensed that their interests were going in different directions. As much as she disliked going out with one egocentric Casanova after another, still there was no other way to find out if perhaps this or that acquaintanceship might be worth developing. It seemed a vicious circle. She went out on a date, hoping to find Mr. Right, only to find Mr. Wrong. But if she didn't give them a chance, then how would she ever know what they were really like?

But it was because of that kind of lonely frustration that Karen had found Stuart so attractive. They had had so much to talk about effortlessly. She found him amusing, highly intelligent, and their common interests had turned a mere dinner into a very entertaining evening. Even when he had been serious, his warmth and compassion had shown through. When he had asked her about her family background, Karen had told him that she'd been raised by foster parents.

"But do you know who your real parents are?" he'd asked, his light brown eyebrows pulling together in concern.

"The Ferriers have told me a little about them. I know their names, of course, and where they live."

"Where?"

"In Paris," she had answered simply.

"And you've never looked them up, gone to see them?"

"What for?" She had smiled at his surprise. "The Ferriers have given me all the love anyone could hope for," she'd explained. "If my parents didn't want me, why should I go out of my way for them? There's more to being a father or mother than just a blood relationship; there's the worry, the tending, the guidance. . . ."

Stuart had leaned back, his hazel eyes studying her with a mixture of admiration and confusion. "You're really quite a remarkable young woman. Is everything in your life so clear, so well thought out?"

Karen had laughed. "Whenever possible," she'd said. "After all, complications arise all around me . . . so I try not to clutter my personal world with a lot of problems that aren't necessary."

"No intrigues, no games?"

"Not if I can help it," Karen had responded. "Naturally I make mistakes and find myself in situations that could have been averted. But if people would just give a moment's thought to what they're doing or letting themselves in for, I'd wager that we'd have a much happier world."

Stuart had smiled, raising his glass of wine in toast. "You're very mature for your years, Karen."

"I had the benefit of good parents."

Now comparing the man she had dined with to the one she had encountered at the lodge, she was once again struck by the difference. However, George would get to the bottom of the matter. He was an excellent detective, well respected among his peers, and if Stuart Macloud was a phony, George wouldn't spare her a detailed report.

Trying to get her mind off Stuart, she sat down and wrote a brief letter to Felix Duprez at the Department of Tourism. She didn't know what his title might be, but she was sure he'd get the letter anyway. Felix had been very helpful to her, as well as to the others, and she didn't want to lose track of him. He'd be lonely once he returned to Paris. Back in his own home, his own routines, the loss of his wife would be very hard on him. If at all possible, if Felix would permit it, she wanted to introduce him to the Kleimers. They would like him, she was certain, and the Kleimers gave very nice, small dinner parties where Felix might make a new circle of friends—people with whom he wouldn't associate his wife.

She had just addressed the envelope and sealed it when she heard the evening paper tossed against her apartment door. Wondering if there was any additional information about the train accident, Karen went over to the door, opened it and picked up the late edition of the news. Unfolding the paper, she saw that the headline concerned a strike in Brittany. She was about to turn the page when a small item toward the bottom of page one caught her eye: TYCOON'S SON DISAPPEARS. Beneath it the article continued:

LONDON (Reuter)—According to informed sources Stuart Macloud, the son of Ian Macloud, the Earl of Hogarth, was expected in Nice five days ago. When he failed to appear, Mario Cagliani— the famed art connoisseur—notified the authorities in Nice. He also requested that they investigate the possibility of a connection between the theft of the mask of Lugalki, reportedly worth close to a million dollars, and Macloud's disappearance.

Witnesses have reported that Mr. Macloud had been aboard the ill-fated Trans Europe Express, but no one has confirmed his whereabouts since. The police are checking into the matter at Tournus and Mâcon, where many of the survivors were taken, and some few still remain. The Earl of Hogarth was not available for comment.

Karen lowered the newspaper, a slight frown creasing her forehead. Stuart had disappeared? But he hadn't! She had spoken with him at the lodge! What devious ploy had he devised this time, she wondered.

She crossed over to the telephone, the paper still clutched in her hand, and dialed George Ferrier. Seconds later he was on the line. "Have you seen this evening's paper," she blurted. "About Stuart?"

George's voice was calm, soothing. "Yes, of course I saw it."

"What do you make of it?" Karen asked impatiently.

"Very little," George replied evenly. "Reads to me as if that Cagliani fellow is trying to pin the blame on anyone he can think of. Surprised he didn't mention you, too."

"But George, I saw and *spoke* with Stuart in Tournus! He hasn't disappeared at all."

"Don't be so certain, Karen. You left there on Friday. What's to say your young man hasn't disappeared since? If, as we suspect, he did indeed steal the mask, he might well have taken a powder and is lying low somewhere."

"But George, that would be foolish. For one thing, it would definitely make him look suspicious. For another, he doesn't *have* to! He's going to be a very wealthy man in his own right once his father passes on. . . ."

"Maybe he doesn't want to wait that long, Karen. But I'll tell you what. Maria and I have been wanting to get away for a couple of days anyway. Maybe we'll make reservations at that lodge in Tournus and drive down. I'll do a bit of snooping while we're there."

"Oh, George! Would you?" She was delighted at the prospect of his personal involvement. Karen knew that he could find out more in ten minutes than most policemen could learn in weeks!

"Of course, dear. First, your happiness means everything to us both. Second, I want this mystery around Macloud's head cleared up quickly before your romantic heart falls in love with a memory."

"I can't keep any secrets from you at all," Karen said with a smile.

"Even if I'd never been a detective, I've known you most of your life," George replied, chuckling. "You were always a fool for stray cats and underdogs," he added.

"If Stuart *is* an underdog," she countered.

"Yes, it's a large 'if,' but we'll get to the bottom of it, Karen. Try to be patient."

"Will you call me the moment you learn anything?"

"I promise on my honor. We'll leave this evening."

She laughed, feeling reassured and better about things, and hung up.

AROUND NOON ON TUESDAY as Karen was putting down the groceries she'd just bought, her telephone rang. "Hello?"

"It's George, Karen. I promised I'd call."

"So soon?" Karen curled up on the davenport, clutching the phone to her ear.

"It didn't take very long to verify a few things," he responded. "But I'm afraid I don't have very good news for you."

"What do you mean," she asked, her fingers tightening around the receiver.

"There isn't a Stuart Macloud registered anywhere in the area and never has been. Your check of the local hospitals stands, too—no Macloud."

"But what does that mean?" she said, worried.

"It means something's very fishy," George replied. "I had already managed to get a good description of him from the receptionist at the Residence Parc Monceau—"

"But I already told you what he looks like," Karen interrupted.

"Through rose-colored glasses, Karen. I wanted an objective description. I spoke with a few of the survivors who are still here and also with some of the casualties in the hospital. He was on the train, that's certain. But no one remembers seeing him here at the lodge."

Karen shook her head, angry and upset. "It was the confusion, George. And there were so many of us just dumped there in the middle of the night. Did you talk to Mrs. Montague?"

"Yes, of course. She dimly remembers someone who vaguely resembles my description but explained that no one was even registered at the desk."

"What about Adela? Doesn't she remember her, either?"

"Oh, yes, Adela she remembers. Said the woman kept complaining about the service."

"Which tells me that Stuart kept a low profile while he was there, right?"

"And might also explain not only why it was she who rented the car, but why he was wearing that bandage around his head. Unless you know someone very well, you're more apt to remember something unusual about a person than his actual looks. It was a good trick, and it worked."

"But then; where is he now?" Her eye fell on the article she had clipped out of the newspaper, and she stared at it as if it held the answer.

"My guess is that he's either gone into hiding, or he's returned to England."

Karen sighed. "So what do we do?"

"Now, honey, don't get discouraged. I've had tougher cases than this one," he reassured her. "I'm going to leave Maria here alone tonight, and I'll catch the afternoon train to Nice. I've made an appointment with that Cagliani fellow, and he's agreed to let me check out his security for the mask. I think if I start at square one, I'll have a better chance of finding out what really happened—to the mask and to Stuart."

"I hope you're keeping a good record of your expenses," Karen said. "Franz Kleimer is a stickler about records."

"So's the police department. Don't worry your pretty little head over it."

"All right, but do stay in touch, please."

"I will, dear."

When they'd hung up, Karen began to pace her living room. She felt helpless and useless. None of it made any sense to her; it just got more and more confusing. Restless, she felt too confined in her small apartment and decided to go for a long walk. Maybe the brisk air would help her think more clearly. Putting away the groceries could wait.

Wandering aimlessly down the Rue de Leningrad, then over to the Rue de Constantinople, to the Rue de Naples, she soon realized that she wasn't very far from the Parc Monceau, where Stuart lived. Even her subconscious was working against her, she thought. Maybe a hot cup of coffee would help, she decided, glancing across the street to a small café.

Moments later she took a small table about halfway down the long, narrow café. It was oppressively hot and steamy so she removed her wool scarf and coat, placing them on the empty chair opposite her. She gave her order to the wizened waiter and played with the aluminum creamer on the table while she waited. Then she began to glance around at the other customers. Off to one corner, reading a copy of *Shipping News*, sat Stuart.

Karen's mouth fell open when she recognized him. His bandage was gone, and he didn't seem as well dressed as he had been on the train, but it was definitely Stuart.

Jumping to her feet and gathering up her coat quickly, she walked over to his table. He looked up, staring at her blankly for a moment, then got up and grinned broadly. "What a delightful surprise!"

"What on earth are you doing here," she asked, half in demand and half in incredulous curiosity. "Especially in a place like this?"

"Having a bite of lunch, as you can plainly see," he replied. "Sit down, Karen, join me," he urged, moving his overcoat to an empty chair nearby.

"Don't you know you've disappeared," she queried, seating herself.

He laughed. "Have I? I seem to be where I thought I was," he said, running his hand through his brown hair.

"Where's your beautiful signet ring," she asked inanely.

"Right here," he answered, showing her his right hand. "I seem to have lost a little weight, and it fits better on this hand now."

"Oh," she responded, sensing that something was terribly wrong but unable to pinpoint it. "Do you come here often?"

Stuart smiled. "It's probably the first time I've ever been to this café. Normally when I'm in town, I have a business lunch or fix myself a little something at my place."

"Did you get my note?" Karen asked casually. She smiled at the old waiter as he brought her coffee to her.

"What note?"

"The one I left for you with the receptionist where you live," she said.

"Oh, never leave anything with her. She's so stupid I don't know how she finds her way to work each day." He pulled out the small menu that was propped between the salt and pepper shakers. "Would you like something to eat?"

Karen shook her head. "Stuart, who is Adela?"

His hazel eyes clouded momentarily, but he swiftly recovered. "A friend of mine. Why?"

"She acts as if she owns you," Karen said, hoping she didn't sound too intrusive.

Stuart chuckled. "In a manner of speaking I suppose you could say that. We're, uh, in business together in a way."

"Is she in Paris now with you?" Karen glanced down at her cup, then lifted her blue eyes to meet his. "I'm sorry, I don't mean to pry, but for my own reasons I'd appreciate your honesty."

"No, she's in Argentina. Why? What's the mystery?"

"Don't you know that Cagliani is trying to make it seem as if you stole the mask of Lugalki?" Her gaze was earnest, hoping he would tell her the truth—*all* of it.

He stiffened visibly, a stern and unpleasant expression in his hazel eyes. "Where did you hear that?" he demanded hotly.

"It was in the paper yesterday. He's alerted the police in Nice, and they allege you've disappeared. Don't you see, Stuart? You're probably in a great deal of trouble. Please go to the police and tell them you're here in Paris, explain that you couldn't possibly have stolen the mask!"

Stuart leaned back in his chair, a strange smile crossing his features. "So they believe I took it, eh?"

"Yes."

Suddenly Stuart broke into laughter, almost uncontrollably. "My oh my," he finally said. "Isn't it interesting what can happen when one tempts fate!"

Chapter 10

After his lunch Stuart suggested that they take in a movie or go to a museum together. He was in very high spirits, and Karen couldn't understand why he was so delighted that the police thought he might have stolen the mask. Wouldn't a responsible person want to dispel such a notion instantly? How could anyone think that being a suspect in a crime was amusing? Yet that's exactly what Stuart seemed to feel.

"I gather your injury has healed," she remarked as he pulled out his wallet and paid the bill.

"Hmm? Oh, yes," Stuart replied nonchalantly. "Now what about it? Want to spend the afternoon with me? I'm at absolute sixes and sevens with nothing to do and no one to do it with."

She gazed at him thoughtfully, trying to figure him out. "Aren't you in Paris on business?" she asked.

"Uh, not really. That is, my father wants me to fly to Geneva to take care of some matters for him, but I'm, well, I'm kind of playing hooky."

"Is that why you're so pleased about being considered a missing person?"

He tilted his head to one side, a bemused expression in his eyes. "Let's not talk about that," he replied lightly. "It's a beautiful day, we're together, and all the rest of that stuff will sort itself out in its own good time."

"Stuart," Karen said, leaning her elbows on the tabletop, "are you sure your injury wasn't more serious than you thought?"

"Why do you ask that?" He stood up, pulling on his heavy winter coat.

Karen had expected that he'd hold her chair for her, even as he had done after dinner that fateful night. But when he didn't, she tried not to show her surprise. "It's just that, well, you don't seem yourself," she finally answered.

He grinned. "You just didn't have a chance to get to know me very well," he answered. "After all we had only a couple of hours together. First impressions are frequently wrong." He stood by, watching her, as she pulled on her coat over her scarf.

Karen turned then, facing him. "The man I met last Wednesday would have helped me with my coat," she said evenly, trying to decipher what was behind his hazel eyes. She wanted to keep any tone of accusation out of her statement, hoping to get through to him, to fathom this other Stuart.

"Oh, sorry," he answered quickly, "I guess I just wasn't paying much attention. Shall we go?" He smiled charmingly at her.

"I don't think I'll accept your invitation, Stuart," she responded slowly. "I'm due back at the gallery tomorrow, and I've got a great deal to do."

"What about dinner, then? You can't just let a handsome eligible bachelor wander the streets of Paris all alone!" He was only half joking, and it showed on his face.

Karen hesitated. She wasn't sure she cared for this other aspect of Stuart's personality...but then, she thought, how could she be sure it wasn't only a temporary change due to his head injury? She had been so very impressed by him that first meeting.... He'd charmed her completely, making her feel that there might be more to their relationship in time. But the man who stood before her now was someone else. Oh, nice enough, she supposed...but lacking the depth, the maturity that had first attracted her. That Stuart, the first one, would never have referred to himself as a handsome and eligible bachelor; he would have...well, maybe he might have said.... *Oh damn! I don't know what Stuart would have said, but it would have been sweet and endearing...not a cocky taunt!*

"Well? How about it?" he prodded.

"All right," she said, giving in. "But it has to be an early night. I have to be at work in the morning."

"That's a deal," he replied, pleased with himself. "Pick you up about seven?"

"Fine. I'll be ready."

He put an arm around her shoulder as they left the café. "Where do you live," he asked.

"On Rue Chaptal, number 210, second floor. It's just off the Place de Clichy."

"Fine, I'll find it. Oh, before I forget," Stuart said once they reached the sidewalk, "let's not get too fancy tonight, eh? Maybe there's a nice little restaurant not too far from your apartment?"

She looked up at him, perplexed. "Yes, a couple of them. Actually there's a new place I've been wanting to try. It's run by an American and called Chet's Place.... They have a totally American menu. I hear it's very reasonably priced and isn't yet well known enough to be overcrowded."

"It sounds great. Till seven, then?"

She nodded, waved and headed back to her apartment, wondering why she had accepted the invitation. Whatever it was that was making Stuart so different, Karen knew only that she had to get to the bottom of the matter. Was it possible to have been so attracted to a man and have been so totally wrong about him? Even the way he had spoken of the receptionist as being stupid seemed completely out of character.

Shaking her head, Karen knew that she simply had to give Stuart another chance. If the man she had met didn't surface during dinner that evening, she would have to admit that she had made an error in her assessment of him. Perhaps, as she had previously thought, he had been on his good behavior only in hopes of finding out how much she was authorized to bid on the mask. But then, she asked herself, what difference could it make if he had planned to steal it anyhow?

And, too, his suggestion to dine someplace nearby— was it to save money? But if so, why? When he had ordered their dinner last Wednesday, everything had been first-class.... What had changed since then? His father might have dismissed him from his job, of course, but if that were the case, wouldn't Stuart have gone straight to England to find something else? Why was he surrounded by so much mystery, so many contradictions?

Well, she would find out later...even if she had to shake the truth out of him.

CHET'S PLACE WAS FAIRLY QUIET, with only about half the tables occupied. The jukebox in the corner near the bar was plaintively wailing some American music. The decor was midfifties malt shop with formica-topped tables and chrome chairs filling part of the space and tall booths ranging down one wall. A long, gleaming bar complete with high swivel stools was a focal point in the room, and behind it traditional soda-fountain equipment shared space with inverted bottles of liquor and sparkling glassware of every kind. The white-coated bartender smiled engagingly at the new arrivals as he vigorously agitated a cocktail shaker. Obviously this establishment catered to a varied clientele.

"Quaint, isn't it?" Karen said as she and Stuart were seated at one of the small tables.

"It seems quite authentic," he answered, looking around. "I could live without that whining on the jukebox though." Stuart grimaced. "Sounds as if they have five minutes to live—and in agony at that!"

"Would you prefer not to stay?" Karen asked, surprised that he didn't seem to like the place at all.

"Oh, no, as long as we're here, we might as well sit it out."

A young waiter approached them at that moment, dressed in a pink striped shirt, narrow-legged blue jeans and tapered shoes. "*Bon soir,* folks," he said. "Something from the bar first?"

Stuart glanced at Karen for her response. "A glass of chablis, thank you," she said.

"I'll have a martini," Stuart said confidently.

"Coming right up," the young man responded.

The waiter returned with their drinks shortly, but when Stuart took a sip from his glass, he frowned then signaled to the waiter. "I asked for a martini," he said.

"Oh, you wanted just vermouth?" The waiter started to reach for the glass, but Stuart stopped him.

"No, no, I'm sorry," Stuart said apologetically. "I guess I temporarily forgot about American martinis. This is fine."

Karen watched him curiously. They had had martinis on the train, and he knew perfectly well what they were. Why had he not recognized the drink? At that moment she was convinced more than ever that his concussion had caused not only a change in his behavior but had also affected his memory. Still she couldn't shake the nagging knowledge that there was no record of Stuart being treated in a single hospital! "Stuart," she said evenly, "do you recall which hospital they took you to in Tournus?"

He looked at her as if the question were an insult, then his light eyes softened. "No, frankly. Why do you ask?"

"Are you sure that it was in Tournus at all? Could they have taken you somewhere else?" She was hoping that he would come up with a town where she hadn't checked. After all it *was* possible that some of the passengers might have been taken to Cluny, or even Borg. Just how reliable was Mrs. Montague's information in the first place?

Stuart seemed mildly irritated. "I really don't remember, Karen. Now are we going to have a pleasant time, or are you going to continue to harp about what happened last week?" He spread his hands on the table and looked down. "Sorry. Didn't mean to be so short-tempered. But let's forget all about what happened that night—other than that we met. All right?"

She smiled wanly. "I just think your injury was worse than they told you, and I think you should see a Parisian doctor first thing in the morning. A specialist, preferably."

"If it will make you happy, I will," Stuart said, lifting his glass to his lips.

"I hate to sound like an old-maid aunt, but did you telephone the police this afternoon to let them know you're in Paris?"

He slapped his forehead lightly. "It completely slipped my mind," he admitted. "Maybe you're right. Maybe I should see a doctor. I normally have a superb memory," he added with a boyish smile.

Pleased that he was beginning to see reason, Karen said, "Why don't you call them now," she suggested. "There must be a pay phone in here somewhere."

"You're right. I'll be right back." He patted her hand and left the table.

She watched him as he stopped a waiter, asked for the phone, then was pointed toward the rest rooms to their right. As he made his way between the tables, a young woman looked up and smiled at him brightly. "Pierre!"

He paused for a moment. "I'm sorry, Miss, you've mistaken me for someone else," Stuart said tersely.

"But Pierre, only last month we—"

"C'mon, Monique, the guy already said you've made a mistake," the woman's escort complained.

She shrugged, then said in a high-pitched, annoyed voice, "But he's a dead ringer for Pierre!"

"So?"

Karen watched the exchange in mild amusement as Stuart disappeared around the corner. She sipped at her wine while she waited for him to return, enjoying the uniqueness of the restaurant's decor as she studied it more closely. It was unquestionably a very clever idea, and she could well appreciate why the American place was gaining in popularity. Now if the cuisine was also good, Karen didn't see how the place could fail to be a huge success.

Their waiter stopped by with two menus, then went on to another table. Karen picked one up and glanced at it curiously: western sandwiches; hot dogs with chili sauce; porterhouse steak; baked potato with sour cream; and at least a half dozen versions of the hamburger, which seemed to be the main feature. She had once tried a cheeseburger at Le Drugstore, but Chet's Place hailed theirs as "genuine," which she supposed meant that what was available at Le Drugstore was not. Fortunately she had always been adventurous about food and liked to try new things whenever she could.

As Karen tried to understand the menu, Stuart returned to their table. "There. All attended to," he said amiably. "See anything interesting on the menu," he asked, picking up his.

"Didn't they want to see you?" she asked.

"Who," he responded, frowning as he read what was available.

"The police," she said.

"Why should they?"

"Because of Cagliani's allegations," she replied.

"Oh that," Stuart said, grinning. "No, I simply explained that I had never reached Nice, and that I was having dinner this evening with someone who could corroborate my statement—you would, wouldn't you?" His gaze was steady, somewhere between a challenge and entreaty.

"Did they ask my name?" she evaded, trying to gather her thoughts.

"Of course, and I gave it to them. Why not?"

"No reason," she said, mustering a smile she didn't quite mean.

Then deftly Stuart changed the direction of their conversation and began to discourse on some of the recent plays he had seen. He was very animated and full of behind-the-scenes anecdotes, and he was surprisingly well informed about the backgrounds of many of the performers. He was so entertaining that Karen practically forgot about everything else until coffee was served. It made her remember that she had to go to work the next day, which she rather regretted. She knew that Stuart liked the theater because he had said so on the train, but she had no idea of just how well versed he was.

Once the bill was paid, Stuart walked back to the Rue Chaptal with her, then up the flight of stairs to her front door. "Will I see you tomorrow?" he asked, standing close to her.

"I—I'm not sure," Karen answered, terribly conscious of his nearness.

"Maybe this will help you make up your mind," he said and took her in his arms.

Stuart's lips lowered to capture hers, and he brought her body snugly against his own. His mouth moved knowingly but roughly. She could feel his response all too easily, and his breathing was becoming ragged as his hands began to knead her lower back.

Knowing full well that things might go too far if she didn't break the kiss, Karen tried to pull away gently. But when it became evident that he wasn't going to let her go, she practically had to push him away.

"What's the matter, baby? Weren't you enjoying it?" His tone was belligerent.

Karen could only stare at him, wondering why he had been so rough with her, so demanding. This was not the kiss she had anticipated, not what she had expected Stuart Macloud to be like! "I'm no one's baby, Stuart," she said somewhat testily.

"Aw, c'mon, you know you liked my kissing you. You've been practically begging for it all evening," he said, then seemed to catch himself. "That wasn't what I meant to say, Karen, forgive me. The truth is that I've wanted to kiss you ever since I first saw you. . . . I guess I got a little carried away. Forgiven?"

He seemed genuinely contrite and she nodded. "Good night, Stuart. Thank you for a lovely evening. . . once again."

He saluted her with a forefinger to his forehead, smiled ruefully, then turned and went down the wooden stairs and out the front door.

Karen stood there for a moment, puzzled still, until she heard the muffled sound of her telephone. Swiftly she entered her apartment and rushed to answer it. It was her foster father.

"I've been trying to reach you all evening," he said.

She smiled into the receiver. "I was out to dinner," she explained, "with Stuart Macloud."

"That's impossible," George said. "I've checked with Scotland Yard, and they confirmed that he's disappeared."

"But he hasn't! He's here in Paris, and he telephoned the police tonight to let them know where he was."

"Are you absolutely positive?" His voice was incredulous.

"Well, I didn't watch him dial the number, but I'm reasonably sure." She could practically see George frowning at the other end of the line. "What did you find out from Mr. Cagliani?"

George made an angry sound. "Like so many rich people he had a security setup for the mask that any five-year-old could've figured out! He might as well have advertised in the paper where the mask was kept."

"Didn't he even have it in a safe?"

"Sure," George remarked sarcastically. "But it's so old that you can easily see the wear marks where the combination has been used over the years." He snorted with wry amusement. "You should've seen his face when I told him the combination to his own safe!"

Karen found it difficult to see the humor in the situation; too much was riding on who had stolen the mask. "Is it possible, George, that Mr. Cagliani is pulling a con game? Could he have stolen his own property?"

"I thought of that, too, honey, and yes, it's an old trick. But he didn't have the mask insured, so there would be no profit in it. No, I believe him. Someone really did steal the mask. The question is who, and where is it now?"

Either in Argentina, or at the Residence Parc Monceau, Karen thought, wishing she could believe otherwise. They exchanged a few more words, and George promised he would call again if he learned anything worthwhile. Otherwise he and Maria would drive back to St. Ouen the following afternoon and be home by early evening.

When Karen got off the line, she sat for a few moments thinking over what George had said. Then impulsively she picked up the receiver and dialed the police headquarters.

"Sergeant Moreau," a man's voice answered in a monotone.

Against her better judgment, not really wanting to hear the answer, Karen asked, "Did you get a phone call from Stuart Macloud about two hours ago?"

"Who?"

"Macloud, the missing son of the English shipping tycoon."

"Hold on, I'll check the logbook." When he came back on the line, he said, "No, lady. No Macloud called here."

"If he reached another precinct, would they relay the information to you?"

"If he's as important as you say, they'd have to report it to headquarters from a different precinct. That, or heads would roll," he said dryly.

"Thank you," Karen said quietly and hung up. She stared vacantly at the opposite wall for a few moments. He had lied to her...but why? How could it possibly benefit Stuart to be suspected of grand theft? Shouldn't he be doing everything in his power to refute such an allegation? Wasn't he hanging himself?

"Oh Stuart...Stuart...." A tear rolled down her cheek as the implications of this new development sank in.

Chapter 11

The Kleimer Gallery was a beehive of activity when Karen returned to work. Jenny seemed to be going in five directions at once, the phones were ringing continually, and if Karen hadn't known better, she would have thought they were mounting a new show that very day.

Karen hung her overcoat in the closet in the hallway that led to the employee kitchen—one of the nice benefits offered by the Kleimers—and almost bumped into Ilse as she turned. "What's all the excitement about?" Karen asked.

Ilse shook her head as if the world had gone mad. "It's the news about our having the Lund exhibit!"

"But why?"

The woman shrugged helplessly. "For such a sophisticated city, the capital of France, people are reacting to the news as if they'd never seen nude studies before."

Karen was surprised. "Because the paintings are mildly erotic?"

Ilse nodded. "You'd think they were pornographic! It's absolutely astounding."

"While it's true that Sven Bergman's work is terribly stylistic in its sensuality...there's nothing 'pornographic' about his paintings. He celebrates love, not carnal decadence," Karen exclaimed indignantly.

"I know," Ilse sighed. "But half of Paris seems to think otherwise." She pushed a strand of gray hair away from her eyes. "Franz is impatient to see you, dear. You had better run upstairs right away." Then she put a staying hand on Karen's arm. "Have you had enough rest?"

Karen smiled. "Yes, quite enough, thanks. What Franz sometimes forgets is that being young is a help to bounce back quickly...but it doesn't mean one is superhuman."

Ilse laughed. "He doesn't mean to be a slave driver, as you know. As long as you continue to stand up to him, he'll see reason."

"I'll go on up now," Karen said, leaving the hallway and heading up the broad stairway.

"Ah," Franz said as she walked in. "Now we can get some real work done around here. It's nice to have you back, Karen," he remarked, his dark brown eyes sparkling beneath his thick gray eyebrows. Then, rubbing his bony hands together, he asked, "Have you heard anything from your foster father?"

She quickly summarized what had transpired while Franz listened intently, occasionally asking questions. "But when I told him that Stuart was right here in Paris, that he hadn't disappeared at all, George was quite surprised."

Franz was stroking the underside of his mustache as he listened. "But he doesn't know yet that Stuart lied to you about phoning the police—correct?"

"Right. But he'll be back in St. Ouen early this evening, and I can tell him then. In the meantime maybe George has learned more about the mask's possible whereabouts."

"Good," the old man responded. "Now about the Lund exhibit. I want you to get to work on it right away. Get as much free publicity as you can from the TV networks. Offer them passes if you wish."

"Franz," Karen reasoned patiently, "you know that I can't bribe these people.... They'd be insulted, and we'd never get a free plug again!"

"All right, all right, but do the best you can. Cultural exchange—Norway's leading artist in Paris for the very first time, that sort of thing."

"What about the press?" Karen inquired.

"They have been phoning us as the word spreads through town. Will Sven Bergman be here in person? When is opening night? Will photographs be permitted? What security measures will be taken? I don't think the discovery of Gauguin's murals caused as much of a stir as Bergman being on display at the Kleimer Gallery!" He chuckled, pleased with himself. "You did a very good job in Oslo, Karen. I'm proud of you. Now go on back downstairs and get to work. We have only three weeks to get the word around."

"That's not enough time, Franz," Karen contradicted vehemently. "You know as well as I do that the major magazines need a lot more lead time than that! I'll need twelve weeks to plant the information with them! They work months in advance!"

"Can you do it in two?"

"I can try, but I won't make any promises."

Franz scowled then suddenly brightened. "All right,

then we might be wise to open the exhibit to our regular patrons only for the first month. They'll think they're getting preferential treatment, and those snobs will be delighted not to rub elbows with the 'commoners.' Yes, that should work out nicely. Then, when we do open our doors to the general public, we'll not only have made the profits from the private viewing, but the word will have traveled, and we'll make twice as much with the public."

Karen had no difficulty envisioning the dollar signs that were ringing up in Franz's mind. "Then you agree that I can have at least two months with the magazines?"

"Yes, yes—why not? It can only work to our advantage. But get the television people interested right away. They'll reach those who never read anything, and that's important."

She smiled slowly. "I've often wondered if nonreaders could possibly be interested in art. It's rather like believing that people who love pinball machines would also be interested in ballet, isn't it?"

Her employer clucked impatiently. "Like all young people you are opinionated and prejudiced," he lectured. "Because I enjoy beef doesn't mean I am not interested in desserts!"

"I see what you mean," she replied contritely. "I guess I just haven't had enough experience yet."

Franz's expression softened considerably. "I believe it was Bernard Shaw who said that youth is wasted on the young. Now off with you! This isn't an institute of higher learning, but an art gallery! And I might add, not a nonprofit one, either."

Laughing, Karen made her exit and went back down-

stairs to the large office she shared with Ilse and Eric
Guzman, when he sometimes had to spend time
authenticating one of their paintings or objets d'art. If
the job were really difficult, he took the work home
with him where he had a special room set up with X-ray
equipment as well as certain chemicals that would
reveal a forged patina, or pigments used in the paint
that couldn't have been available at the time of the artist's life. Usually, however, Eric could discern fakes
with a strong light and a magnifying glass.

One time in particular, Karen recalled, he had been
able to tell a forgery simply by the painting's brush
strokes. "Do you see the way the paint has been layered
on here," he had asked her. "The artist's pressure with
the brush is heavier at the bottom than at the top—see
that?"

"Yes," Karen had replied, puzzled.

"That means that whoever painted this landscape was
right-handed. Here, too, with the vertical strokes, the
paint is heavier on the right than on the left. A right-
handed person's pressure forces excess paint on the
brush to squeeze more to the bottom and to the right."

"But what has that to do with the authenticity of this
work?"

Eric had gazed at her solemnly. "The original artist,
the real one, was left-handed!"

She had been deeply impressed, and Eric's knowledge
of such matters never ceased to amaze her. But now she
had more urgent matters to worry about. She started off
by telephoning as many magazines in Paris as she could,
particularly those with columns that gave an agenda of
coming events. She would follow up the phone call with
a news release, but her primary effort was to be sure

that all the local magazines were alerted to include the information. With so little time to work before the exhibit opened, Karen knew she would be lucky if they could run the notice the same month as the exhibit; getting any advance publicity from monthly magazines was practically out of the question.

As soon as the job was done, she started to telephone the local television and radio stations. They had to be handled differently. Stung by entrepreneurs in the past, these people were wary of being drawn into providing unpaid advertising. Karen had to be certain to say the phrase "community service" frequently . . . and even at that, less than half the stations approached agreed to make any mention of the forthcoming exhibit.

By noon her hand felt as if it would never unclench from the telephone, and she was certain she had a callous on her dialing finger. "Well, that was a good morning's work," she said, leaning back in her swivel chair and stretching.

"Are you going to have lunch with us today, or are you going out," Ilse asked absently, sealing the letter she had just typed.

Karen stared at the silent telephone. "I think I'll go out today. A little exercise would do me good, I'm sure."

"Jenny will be disappointed," Ilse commented, amused. "She's been dying to get all the details of the train accident from you firsthand. You've reached celebrity status in her eyes," she added.

Karen smiled. "Like the only survivor of the *Titanic*?"

"Something like that."

"Well, not today," Karen said, picking up her handbag and heading down the hall to get her overcoat.

As she was walking back to the foyer, she observed a familiar figure examining their current exhibit. It was Stuart. Her initial response was to be glad...but subtly another reaction surfaced. Why was he hanging around the gallery? Was he—as George would put it—casing the joint? *Now just stop that*, she admonished herself. But somehow, Karen just didn't feel as comfortable about Stuart as she had when they first met. Ever since that morning in the lodge Karen had had a nagging feeling that Stuart was interested in her for one thing only...and his rough kiss last night had forced her to admit it to herself. It was the last thing she would have believed about him or wanted to believe now...but once the notion had taken firm shape in her mind, there was no erasing it.

Karen just didn't know what to make of Stuart Macloud anymore! And it angered her as well as made her feel like a fool. Then she remembered what her foster mother had taught her. Maria had always told Karen, even when she was a little girl, that anger was often misdirected. "You can think you are angry with someone," she would say, "but actually you're angry with yourself. It is far easier to blame others than it is to accept that we've made a mistake or were stupid and blind."

And she supposed this advice was holding true now with Stuart. She had expected him to be one thing, and he was turning out to be another. But whose fault was that? Her own, she had to admit reluctantly. It wasn't Stuart's responsibility that she had given him certain attributes he didn't seem to possess later. Still it saddened her. She had had such an instant liking for him! *Obviously*, she thought, *my disappointment is dispro-*

portionate.... I let my hopes get too high, and it's my own fault! Having sorted through to that admission, Karen saw that she was being very unfair to Stuart. She was taking her feelings out on him, and that wasn't right.

Then, too, even if Stuart would not prove to be the man she had hoped, still there was the matter of the mask. If they were ever to recover it, she was in the best position to find out where it was.

At that moment Stuart turned and spotted her looking at him. "I hoped to catch you before lunch," he said. "If you don't have a date, why not join me?"

"I only have an hour," she answered, trying to seem pleased by his invitation.

Stuart shook his head gravely. "You've got to stop putting time limits on me," he commented lightly.

Karen smiled. "It's the fate of any salaried employee," she explained. "Perhaps, since you work for your father, you have more freedom on the job than I do. Or maybe it's because you're an executive...but the working classes aren't that privileged."

Stuart gave an exaggerated sigh of resignation. "Very well, then. One hour." He glanced at his watch. "I will have you back here at precisely 1:04 P.M."

She bit back the temptation to tell him that he'd lied to her before. Karen didn't want to risk alienating him. Her best course of action now was to play along with Stuart in hopes that it would give George enough time to discover who had stolen the mask of Lugalki and locate it—if it wasn't too late already.

WHEN KAREN GOT HOME from work that evening, George was waiting for her at the top of the stairs. His rugged features were wearing their "official" look.

"Good news or bad?" Karen asked after giving him a peck in greeting and opening the door to her apartment.

"Too soon to tell," he said seriously, closing the door after them. "But what I've found out is better said in person than over the telephone."

"Oh, George, you always think everyone's line is tapped," Karen said, only half teasing. But the fact was that he wasn't home with Maria at that hour of the evening told her that he'd found out something quite important. "May I get you a glass of wine?" she asked as he removed his coat and folded it neatly over the back of her only armchair.

"Yes, thanks, that would be nice. I've had a long day."

Crossing over to the small bar in the corner, Karen opened the only good bottle of wine she had on hand and poured a glass for each of them. She handed one to George, saying, "Aren't you going to tell me what you've found out?"

"Sit down, dear," he said evenly. He walked over to her living-room window and stood looking down at the street as if verifying that no one had followed him.

"Don't keep me in suspense, George. . .please."

He turned away from the window and gazed at her seriously. "Through Interpol we've run a check on Adela, or Iris Calderón," he began carefully. "She has several other names she's used over the years, but Calderón is the latest one."

"Which suggests that she's been in trouble with the law along the line," Karen responded.

George sipped his wine and sat down on the couch next to her. "She is a very, very clever woman," he said. "The Argentinian authorities have quite a file on her.

Adela was born to a high-ranking minister during the regime in Buenos Aires that followed Perón's exile. When she was still a teenager, that government was ousted when Héctor J. Cámpora was elected president, vowing that he would bring Perón back to power. When he succeeded, he resigned the presidency."

"How did this affect Adela?" Karen wanted to know.

Her foster father shrugged. "We can only guess about the psychological effects. But her father was an arch-enemy of Perón's, and he took his family to Montevideo in Uruguay for safety. Unfortunately he was unable to take any of their possessions other than clothes or personal jewelry, so their life in Uruguay was quite Spartan in comparison with the grandeur they had enjoyed before."

Karen was listening intently, realizing that such a profound change in a teenager's life was bound to have a psychological impact. "What happened next?"

George cocked his head as if the answer should be evident. "Adela used her father's former prestige to worm her way into Uruguayan society, and eventually she married a wealthy petroleum industrialist. He divorced her after a year."

"Not a very happy story," Karen commented sincerely.

"No, but that's probably why she turned to a life of crime. A series of major jewel thefts occurred shortly thereafter, and by then Adela had returned to Argentina. With Perón dead, she either wanted to return to her native country—or perhaps felt that the police were getting wise to her *modus operandi*—which, in truth, was the case. The authorities in Montevideo were pretty certain she was the mastermind of a ring of jewel thieves but didn't have enough proof to press charges. They had no choice but to let her leave the country."

"And then what?"

"She moved to England, but has maintained an elegant apartment here in Paris on the Avenue Foch. However, Interpol is pretty confident that she has switched from jewelry to works of art. Two paintings by masters have turned up in Buenos Aires, and they believe she's smuggling them to contacts in South America."

Karen shook her head. "That's a pretty big enterprise then," she said. "You know then that she's now in Argentina? For all we know she took the mask of Lugalki with her!"

George's expression clearly indicated a grudging admiration. "Maybe. But the question is how? Two pounds of solid gold would be easily detected by airport scanners."

"Perhaps she mailed it to herself, filling out the customs form that the parcel contained books."

"Would you take that risk? I worry about my pension check in the mails between Paris and St. Ouen! But to trust the mail with a package that's worth nearly a million dollars—no, I don't think so. I think the mask is still in Paris."

They each fell silent for a moment. "Then your thinking is that somehow Adela met up with Stuart in England, and together they planned the theft? That Ian Macloud isn't involved?"

"Well, it certainly begins to look that way. Of course, there's nothing to say that they won't try to sell it to the earl. From what your boss has said, I don't think that buying stolen goods would bother Ian Macloud one bit."

"Or," Karen began, thinking swiftly, "it may be a perfect joining of forces. Adela engineers the thefts...but through his knowledge of where their oil tankers are headed, Stuart could easily smuggle almost anything on board."

"Of course," George said, slamming a fist into his palm. "That has to be it! Why didn't I think of it! It's a perfect way to smuggle items out of Europe and ship them to Argentina or anywhere else!"

Karen glanced down at her hands, thinking. In a way she was happy that George was getting closer to a solution to the crime...but she couldn't help being worried that Stuart was so obviously involved in nefarious dealings. What a shame! If only Stuart could have waited to inherit legally from his father...but then she recalled his anecdote about being in and out of the elder Macloud's will. No wonder Adela wanted to keep Stuart all to herself! Without him how would she get the stolen goods out of the country? He was essential to her operation!

"Penny for your thoughts," George said softly. "Though I think I can pretty well guess what they are. You're terribly disappointed about young Macloud, aren't you?" he asked, reaching over and taking her hand in his big paw. "Honey, in times like these, no matter what anyone says, it always seems like a cliché. But aren't you much better off knowing the truth about this young man?"

She gazed up into his searching eyes. "I know, I know...it's just that, well, sometimes I worry that I must have the poorest judgment about men in all the world! I hadn't fallen in love with Stuart quite yet, George, but I wanted to. I can see that now. Am I doomed always to be attracted to the wrong men?"

George pulled her closer and put his arm around her solicitously. "C'mon, put your head on my shoulder and have a good cry. You'll meet the right man one of these days, Karen. He's out there somewhere, waiting to meet you, too."

"I feel like such a dunce," Karen said, wishing she could cry yet knowing she wouldn't. "Maybe I should run an ad in the newspaper: Poor judge of character seeks suitable mate."

George chuckled. "You've plenty of time, honey. You're only twenty-four. Stuart Macloud appealed to the romantic in you, that's all. Handsome young Englishman, titled, wealthy. It was a Prince Charming fantasy that swept you off your feet, not the man."

"I suppose you're right, George. You and Maria are always so good to me, no matter how much trouble I make for you."

"Trouble?" George sat up straight and held her at arm's length. "As a police detective I know what trouble is, Karen. I've seen countless youngsters—from good families as well as bad—hooked on drugs, wasted; I've been at the morgue when they pull out the poor confused kids who have committed suicide because they can't cope with the world. I've watched as youths have been brought in on murder or manslaughter charges. Trouble?" He grinned at her lovingly. "You've been our greatest source of happiness, Karen. And don't you forget that, not ever!"

Chapter 12

Around nine o'clock that evening Karen's telephone rang. Turning the volume down on her small black-and-white TV set, she picked up the receiver. "Yes?"

"Is this Karen Stockwell?" a mature female voice asked.

"Speaking," she answered, wondering what it was all about.

There was a brief pause. "This is Lady Macloud speaking—Stuart's mother."

Surprised, Karen blurted, "Phoning from England?"

The woman sounded faintly amused. "Yes, but let's not worry about that, Miss Stockwell. I'm phoning to find out where my son is."

"Why, he's in Paris. I had lunch with him just today."

"But I don't understand," Lady Macloud exclaimed, obviously taken aback. "Not even an hour ago I received a phone call from Stuart. It was a direct-dial call with no operator assistance. When I picked up on my personal line, I recognized his voice instantly. All he said was: 'Mother—contact Karen Stockwell in Paris. She'll help us. I can't say any more.' And then he hung up abruptly as if someone was coming into the room."

The woman was clearly distraught, and Karen's heart went out to her. "Lady Macloud, I can tell you honestly that Stuart is fine and right here in Paris. While I hesitate to say this, he seems to be playing some sort of a game with everyone."

"What do you mean, Miss Stockwell?"

Karen hated to tell Stuart's mother what was going on, but if she didn't, the poor woman would worry needlessly. She had to tell the truth. "The Paris papers carried an item about Stuart's disappearance; it was in the Monday edition. Then on Tuesday, quite by accident, I ran into Stuart in a small café."

She was hesitant to tell the woman everything yet felt it would be grossly unkind not to. "Are you also familiar with the theft of the mask of Lugalki, stolen from Mr. Cagliani in Nice?"

Lady Macloud laughed lightly. "By all means, Ian—my husband—is livid about it!"

Which meant, Karen reasoned quickly, that the earl hadn't been approached yet to buy it . . . or that he was a very good actor. "Well, the report here is that Stuart might have been implicated in the theft."

"That's preposterous!"

Karen lifted her shoulders, wishing she could agree, but she already knew too much to believe in Stuart's innocence. However, she didn't want to heap one worry in place of another, so she said instead, "There's no concrete evidence, of course. But when I had dinner with Stuart last night, I pleaded with him to notify the authorities of his presence in Paris."

"Pleaded?" Lady Macloud asked in a shocked tone. "He should have presented himself instantly, the moment the news appeared."

Karen had to smile. "I totally agree, Lady Macloud. But he didn't seem to be aware of the news item, and when I told him about it on Tuesday, he laughed uproariously."

"My son actually thought it was funny?" Her voice was incredulous as if they were talking about two different people.

"I'm afraid so. But there's something even stranger about his behavior."

"Go on, Miss Stockwell. I have been sick with worry, and I appreciate your candor."

Then Karen told her about Stuart lying about phoning the police in Paris. "He actually seems to be enjoying the whole thing, Lady Macloud."

"I see," the older woman remarked seriously. Then, taking a different tone, she said, "I can tell from your voice that you care about my son, Miss Stockwell. I appreciate your concern, please believe that." She paused for a second. "Is there more to what's going on? Something you're holding back from me?"

Karen wrestled with the question momentarily. "Only that Stuart's refusal to go to the police could compromise him with the stolen mask." She didn't want to say anything about his alleged concussion or the lack of any records to prove it. That was too much.

"Just how serious is his position in this matter?" Lady Macloud asked in a no-nonsense tone.

"I'm not qualified to answer that question," Karen replied carefully. "But certainly it does make him a suspect unless he goes to the authorities and explains himself."

"But surely he realizes that! What on earth is wrong with that boy!"

Karen shook her head. "I don't know, Lady Macloud. But you should talk to him directly, try to make him see reason. It's clear that he doesn't intend to take my advice. Maybe he'll take yours."

"Yes, perhaps I will. I dislike interfering in Stuart's life as a rule. However, this is no trivial matter. I'll phone him at his residence right away."

"May I ask a favor?"

"Certainly, what is it?"

"When you speak to him would you call back to let me know what he said? I don't understand why he's behaving so strangely...much less his cryptic phone call to you this evening. I want to believe in your son, Lady Macloud, but he's making it very difficult."

"He may be out," the woman said, her tone suddenly soft and understanding. "How late may I call you?"

"I'll wait up for your call, Lady Macloud," Karen stated simply.

The other woman's voice was sympathetic as she asked, "Does Stuart know that you care this much?"

"I thought he should have guessed," Karen answered honestly. "Apparently I was wrong. And now that he's acting so strangely...I no longer know what I feel about him."

"Your forthrightness is most refreshing, Miss Stockwell, and I appreciate it," she said briskly. "And by the way, please call me Maggie.... I'm an American, and I don't have much use for all these titles. I only used it when I phoned in case this was some kind of a hoax."

"Thank you, Lady—Maggie." It felt very strange to be speaking to a countess and asked to use her first name. "I'll wait for your call," Karen said and replaced the receiver gently.

Had she revealed too much, Karen wondered. After all, Lady—Maggie was bound to know that she hardly knew her son; had met, in fact, only one week before. But Karen liked the woman, her frankness and efficiency. Given only a name and a city, obviously Maggie had simply dialed Information for the number. There was only one other Stockwell in the Paris directory—Karen's parents—so it couldn't have been too much trouble. However, few people ever thought to do the obvious. Maggie Macloud was a sensible, direct woman, and Karen admired her for that. That didn't mean, though, that Stuart's mother would be so happy about his involvement with an assistant in an art gallery. "What involvement?" Karen asked aloud, annoyed with herself.

There I go again, she chastised, *putting more into our first meeting than was there!*

She sat down on the armchair next to the end table with the telephone and picked up the book she had been reading before her trip to Oslo. Written by a leading authority, it was a guide to buying art as a hedge against inflation. . .something Karen believed she should know about when dealing with clients at the gallery.

Unable to concentrate fully, Karen took a pack of cigarettes from her handbag and hoped smoking would help calm her nerves. While she had a great deal of patience in many areas, waiting to find out what was happening, tied to the telephone, wasn't one of them. It was different when she could go somewhere, do different things to take her mind off the silence . . . but confined to her apartment, expecting the phone to ring at any moment, wasn't her idea of fun.

Sighing, she picked up the book and again tried to glean the useful information from it. Karen glanced at her watch. It was 9:10. Maybe Stuart's line was busy . . . or even as Maggie had predicted, he wasn't home. Had Stuart mentioned anything during lunch about having to go out this evening? She was certain he hadn't, but that didn't mean his plans couldn't have changed. Or maybe he just felt it was none of her business . . . which would be true enough.

Karen got up and checked the wall clock in her small kitchen. It was now 9:20. Her watch was correct. "This is like waiting for the pot to boil," she muttered to herself, deciding that she might as well do just that by lighting the burner beneath the dented and chipped kettle. A hot cup of chamomile tea might soothe her nerves while she waited.

Finally just before half past nine, Maggie called her back. "There's something very amiss, Karen—may I call you that?"

Karen nodded as if the woman could see her consent. "What did you learn?"

"I spoke to the receptionist in the lobby when Stuart didn't answer his telephone. She said she hadn't seen him since last Wednesday."

"But that's impossible! He's right here!"

"I then talked to the manager of the residence, and he confirmed it. There are several messages for him at the switchboard, and some mail he hasn't picked up."

Karen frowned, trying to assimilate the news. "But if he isn't at his residence, where could he be?"

"More importantly," Maggie responded thoughtfully, "why hasn't he gone to his own apartment?" She hesitated briefly. "I may be his mother, but I'm not a fool. It almost looks as if Stuart is hiding out, not wanting to be found by anyone. Tell me, Karen, is it really possible that Stuart might have stolen that mask?"

Karen hated to be cornered, so she hedged. "Yes, but as my foster father pointed out, so could a lot of other people...including me."

"Mind you," Maggie said, "I don't believe for an instant that Stuart would be capable of such a thing. But he did have a fierce row with his father about making the trip to Nice, and perhaps...well...could he have done something like that as a joke?"

There was such concern in Maggie's voice that Karen didn't know how to reply. She looked down at the book in her lap, and spoke slowly. "It would be pretty extreme, don't you think?"

"You mentioned your foster father.... How is he connected with what's happening?"

As casually as she could, Karen explained that George had been hired by the Kleimer Gallery to find the mask. "Once he's done that," she added hastily, "I'm sure that Stuart will be cleared of all suspicion."

"Would it be all right if I were to speak to your foster father?"

"I only wish I could say yes," Karen answered, genuinely regretful. "But he's on retainer by Franz Kleimer.... I don't think he could betray the confidentiality of the case. I can give you George's phone number, of course, but I don't want to mislead you."

"You're probably right," Maggie said, disappointed. "All right, Karen, we'll just have to take matters into our own hands. I'll have to tell Ian what's happened, naturally, but I have a feeling in my bones that the resolution to this mystery will end up in our hands, yours and mine. I'm going to give you the number to my private line, and if you learn anything at all about what's going on . . . may I count on you to telephone me? Collect, of course."

"I'm in a rather awkward position," Karen responded guardedly. "As an employee of Mr. Kleimer and as the confidante in George's investigations, I'm afraid—"

"I understand," Maggie interrupted, grasping the situation instantly. "Then, may I ask you to call if it pertains to Stuart's safety? You may refrain from offering any information other than that he's all right, or he's in jeopardy. Is that fair?"

"But he *is* all right, Maggie . . . unless something has happened between one o'clock this afternoon and now."

"Then why hasn't he gone to his apartment? Why that strange telephone call this evening to contact you? No, my dear, something is seriously wrong . . . and I'll need your help."

"All right, Maggie, I'll call if I learn anything."

There was an audible sigh at the other end. "Thank you, Karen. I only hope that whatever's wrong with Stuart, that we're not too late to help him!"

THE TELEPHONE CONVERSATION with Maggie Macloud nagged Karen all the next morning. Ilse and Franz had noticed her agitation but had refrained from saying anything about it. However, the more Karen thought about both the receptionist and the manager saying that Stuart hadn't been seen since last Wednesday, the more she wondered if he hadn't put them up to it.

Since the gallery was quite near the Parc Monceau, Karen decided to take a walk up there during her lunch hour. With any luck at all she might run into the same loquacious receptionist and get more information out of her.

"I may be a few minutes late getting back," Karen told Ilse as she put on her coat.

"It's an utterly beautiful day, Karen," the older woman exclaimed. "Don't you have something lighter to wear? A sweater, perhaps?"

"Not here at the gallery," she said. "But if I get too warm, I can just carry my coat. It's still winter, after all."

"True," Ilse conceded. "But spring is in the air, Karen. Soon the trees along the Champs-Elysées will begin to bud, and we'll be putting the snow and slush behind us. And of course, it means so much to Franz when he can be carried downstairs so I can wheel him to the park. While winter for all of us is a nuisance, for him it's a prison."

Karen wished that Ilse hadn't used the word "prison," but tried not to let it show on her face. Instead she smiled and with a slight wave let herself out of the gallery and began to walk briskly up the Avenue Hoche. True to Ilse's prediction she was entirely too warm, and she shed her coat as she hurried past the Boulevard de Courcelles.

In a very short while she was stepping on the carpeting before the glass doors of the Residence Parc Monceau and was relieved to see the same young woman at the desk. "Hello, there," Karen said airily. "I was here on Sunday and left a note for Mr. Macloud...do you remember?"

"Why yes, of course," she responded, smiling warmly.

"I was wondering, since I haven't heard from him, if he has returned to Paris." She tried to sound casual, showing only friendly interest.

The girl shook her head apologetically. "I'm afraid not. But his stays here are never very predictable. He could show up this afternoon . . . or not for another three weeks. I'm sure he'll telephone you the moment he picks up his messages. Mr. Macloud is a very proper gentleman, after all."

"Well," Karen said cheerfully, "I just thought I'd check. I was in the neighborhood anyway," she fibbed.

"Did you want to leave another message?" the receptionist inquired pertly, picking up the others in his cubicle.

"No, no . . . I was merely curious, that's all. Thanks again," Karen said, leaving the lobby and crossing over to the park.

What they had told Maggie was true, that was clear. Stuart had not returned to his apartment. But why? She strolled slowly across to the park, trying to figure out what he was up to. Once again on the Avenue Hoche, just past the Japanese Embassy, Karen's attention was caught by a white Rolls-Royce parked across the street. A uniformed chauffeur was leaning against the front fender, talking to the doorman of one of Paris's better restaurants. She stopped, wondering if it could be . . . ?

Rather than risk a stupid mistake, Karen jaywalked the avenue, purposefully striding toward the restaurant's double doors as if she were quite late for a luncheon date.

The doorman tipped his cap and held the door open

for her. She smiled her thanks as she glanced at her watch and entered the elegantly appointed establishment. A maître d' came toward her, a happily expectant look on his face. "Miss?"

Karen frantically searched for something to say. She couldn't very well claim to be meeting anyone; if she did, he'd show her to the table, and all would be lost. A sense of mounting excitement crept up her spine, and she gestured him over to one side. She motioned for him to lower his head, then whispered conspiratorially, "I'm with *Paris Match*, we've a tip that the Argentinian socialite Iris Calderón is in town...and that certainly looks like her Rolls. It would be quite a scoop for me," Karen lied, pulling out some money and placing it in the man's hand, "if you'd confirm that she's here."

He assessed the denomination of the bill with the practiced glance of a poker player scanning his hand, then nodded briefly. "Wait here, miss, while I check our reservations."

Impatiently she watched him at the rostrum, running his finger down the large, lined ledger beneath the lighted brass lamp. Karen couldn't imagine what was taking him so long until she stole a glance around the potted ferns. The place was infinitely larger than it would have seemed from the outside, seating at least 200 or more diners. Under the circumstances she could understand that Adela's alias might not be at the top of the luncheon reservation list.

Finally he came over to her. "Yes, she and her guest are at table seventy-eight."

"Her guest?"

The maître d' drew himself up to full height as if he had already earned his tip and really didn't have to divulge anything else. "I wasn't given his name. Tall, brown hair, light eyes—probably English, I'd say."

"Thank you," Karen said quickly. "I'll try to get one of our photographers over here to catch them on their way out," she said, praying lightning wouldn't strike her dead. She gave him an ingratiating smile and left the restaurant. Well, in for a penny, in for a pound, she thought, digging into her purse for some more money...hoping against hope that Franz would reimburse her.

Still smiling, she went up to the chauffeur and, slipping him the money, gave him the same story about being with the famous French magazine. "I know that Iris Calderón is inside," she said, pulling the driver by the sleeve and away from the doorman. "I'm wondering if you could tell me who her luncheon guest is."

The chauffeur shrugged and handed the money back to her. "I really don't know. Miss Calderón only met him about a month ago, I'd say. But she's certainly never introduced him to *me!*"

"Don't you have even a hint?"

"Sorry. I only know that he lives not too far from the Gare de l'Est in the tenth district. I've been dispatched to pick him up a couple of times—despite the fact that I've warned Miss Calderón about that neighborhood. So I don't have to leave the car unattended, he's waited for me out in front."

Karen frowned, folding the bills back into her purse. "Well, thanks anyway," she said and walked away. She was deep in thought as she strolled down the Avenue Hoche toward the Rue du Faubourg St. Honoré and then stopped in her tracks. The description of the man with Adela was too close to Stuart's to ignore. But the chauffeur had said that this man lived in a rather run-down section of Paris.... Why would Stuart have two apartments?

Then it occurred to her that he might have a split personality, and one didn't know what the other was up to...but that was far too unlikely. While Karen knew very little about such things, the few cases she had read about in magazines and the papers indicated a radical change when one personality took over the other. A quiet person would become bois-terous; a peaceful one would turn aggressive or vio-lent. She had even read about alterations in how they dressed, or, particularly with women, how they wore their hair.

Granted, Stuart had shown a change from when she had first met him, but nothing as dramatic as she would expect if he were genuinely mentally ill.

Perplexed but determined, Karen found a pay tele-phone and called the gallery. "Ilse," she said, "something has come up that may take the rest of the afternoon to resolve. Could I have the time off?"

"But Karen, dear, you only got back to work yester-day...and there's the Lund exhibit! Whatever could I tell Franz so he wouldn't be angry?"

"I know it's asking a great deal, Ilse," Karen said half-guiltily, "but this is terribly important. I may be onto something that will help us locate the mask. Surely that's more important to Franz than my being gone a few hours."

"Well, dear, I really don't know what to say. Does your foster father know what you're up to? Shouldn't you let him handle whatever it is you've come across?"

"There's no time, Ilse. He couldn't possibly get here

before . . . well, it's just something I have to follow up on my own. Please?"

Ilse let out a relenting laugh. "Why do I have the distinct impression you're going to take the time with or without my permission?" she said.

"You won't regret it, Ilse, I promise. Bye now!" Karen hung up quickly before the woman could change her mind, then walked to the branch office of her bank to cash a check. She doubted that she would have enough money otherwise.

Coming back outside, Karen hailed a taxi and gave him the name of the restaurant where Adela was.

"But that's just a block from here, lady," he complained. "You could walk it faster than I can get through this traffic!"

Feeling like some kind of modern Mata Hari, Karen leaned forward waving her purse. "There's a white Rolls-Royce parked in front. You're going to park at a discreet distance, and we'll wait for the owner to come out. I'll recognize her and probably the man she's with. If the man gets in the car with her, you're to follow the Rolls until he gets out. Then you'll take me to the Rue Chaptal."

"Look, lady, if they're having lunch in there, we could be sitting for a couple of hours! I don't make any money if my meter isn't on, and I've got a family to support!"

"Leave it on," Karen said. "I wouldn't dream of asking you to do this without making money. Besides, we don't know. Maybe they came here for an early lunch. They might leave the restaurant at any moment!"

The driver lifted his leather cap off his forehead and scratched his head, then he threw down the lever on the meter. "Okay, lady, it's your nickel!"

Chapter 13

An hour and a half later Adela emerged from the restaurant, squinting at the afternoon sun. She seemed in a very good mood, laughing gaily as she clung to Stuart's arm.

Karen tapped the driver on the shoulder, suddenly aware that he'd been dozing. "There they are," she told him.

"Are you a policewoman or something?" the driver asked, rubbing his eyes.

"In a manner of speaking," Karen replied. "I'm working with them on a case." *And that's not too far from the truth*, she told herself.

She watched as the chauffeur opened the rear door, and both Adela and Stuart climbed in. As the driver walked around to his side of the car, the cabby started up his engine. "Just follow them," Karen reminded him. "But not too close!"

"What if they're going to the airport or out to the country?" he asked, already anticipating the worst.

"Did you see any luggage? Any indication that they had anything more than a luncheon date?"

"I ain't Sherlock Holmes, lady."

"Don't worry. I think you'll find that they'll go to the tenth district first.... After that we don't care where the Rolls goes."

Because the English car was so wide, the chauffeur couldn't take advantage of the more direct side streets but kept to the broader avenues. About a half hour later the Rolls was cutting across to the Boulevard de Magenta and shortly thereafter turned into the dead-end Avenue de Verdun.

Karen had been able to observe, depending on where the sun was glinting off the rear window, that Stuart had his arm around Adela. It cut Karen deeply to realize that he might be having an affair with that woman yet had the nerve to ask her out for dates when Adela was out of the country. But Karen also knew that she had to keep her personal feelings out of it. This was no time for sorrow over what might have been. Instead she had to find out exactly where Stuart was staying. After that she would ask George to follow through.

The white Rolls pulled over in front of a rather run-down building. Stuart climbed out of the car, then leaned back in to give Adela a kiss. She slapped his face playfully, then gestured to the chauffeur to drive on.

"Now what, lady?" the cabby inquired.

"Rue Chaptal, number 210," she answered as she quickly wrote down the number of the building Stuart had entered. While it wasn't truly a slum area, it certainly wasn't the sort of neighborhood where she'd expect to find a man of his background. But then, perhaps that was the point, she thought grimly.

Karen went over all the events leading up to the present as the driver took her home. There wasn't a doubt in her mind that George would be quite interested in this latest development, and she planned to telephone him the moment she was inside her apartment. What particularly piqued Karen's curiosity was why Adela was so blatantly present in Paris, while Stuart didn't wish to be seen at his own home. Even if he were her accomplice in crime, wouldn't it look less suspicious if he maintained a "life-as-usual" facade?

The driver pulled up, and she shelled out a hefty tip in addition to what it read on the meter. Most drivers, she knew, would have refused her as a fare, preferring to get many passengers for the additional tip. She thanked him and got out of the taxi, already mentally dialing George's telephone number.

When she unlocked her apartment door, Karen was startled to see a woman standing by the windows overlooking the street. Slowly she turned and a little smile creased her face. In her mid- to late fifties, she was dressed simply but in impeccably good taste. Her hair was short and wavy, in color a rich dark brown with glints of silver. Her facial features were patrician, dominated by very large green eyes.

The woman broke into a broader smile. "I'm afraid I lied to the manager," she said quietly. "I told him I was your aunt, just in from the United States."

There could be no question. The physical resemblance was too great. Karen closed the door and crossed the room to accept the extended hand. "I'm delighted to meet you, Maggie," she said sincerely. "But, if I may ask, why are you here?"

Maggie took a long look at Karen. "You're even lovelier than I expected. Stuart has excellent taste, I must say." She moved toward the davenport. "May I sit down?"

"Of course," Karen said, still waiting for an explanation. She watched Lady Macloud lower herself gracefully, but she remained standing expectantly as if to coax an answer from the older woman.

"I tried telephoning you all morning," Maggie said. "Then I realized that you probably had a job. Not knowing where you worked and keenly aware that we don't have a moment to lose, I flew out of London on the first available plane."

"What's happened, Maggie?" Karen asked warily, already conscious that she wouldn't like the answer.

Maggie opened her handbag and gave Karen a piece of paper folded in quarters. "Perhaps you had better sit down, Karen."

She had the message half unfolded as she took the facing armchair, then with disbelieving eyes she read:

If you ever want to see your son alive, you will deposit £1,000,000 sterling to the account of Stuart Macloud, at Lloyds Bank on Oxford Street. The money is to be in cash, small bills, and must be deposited no later than closing time tomorrow. Failure to do so will result in your son's death. Contacting the police would be futile.

Karen looked up at Maggie in amazement. "But this is absurd! I just saw Stuart entering a seedy apartment house!"

Maggie's expression was drawn and serious. "Can we afford to take any risks, Karen?"

Numbly, still trying to grasp what it all meant, Karen went to the telephone. "I'll ask George to come right over," she said. "Someone is pulling a hoax or a double double-cross!"

GEORGE FERRIER RUBBED HIS CHIN thoughtfully as he listened to Karen and Lady Macloud. They had already shown him the ransom note, which he had put in his pocket to take to the lab—to determine, if possible, whether the typewriter used had been of English or French manufacture. The envelope in which it had been delivered had no postmark; whoever had sent it had used a messenger service in London. Naturally Maggie hadn't thought to ask which service, nor had she noticed any name on the car that had been used. Why should she? Deliveries were made all the time, and she had had no reason to think this one was going to be any different.

"You say you saw him enter an apartment building on Avenue de Verdun," George asked, pulling out a pencil and notepad.

"Right," Karen confirmed.

"Why would Stuart want to do this?" Maggie asked, on the verge of tears. "I can only believe he's temporarily mad, pretending to have been abducted in order to bilk his own parents for a million pounds! What's happened is so terribly unlike my son that it's laughable," she concluded, vainly trying to smile. "And then this . . . this alleged nonsense about his involvement with the stolen mask!"

George's expression clearly indicated that he was at a loss for words to comfort this woman he had just met, and Karen could only empathize. How does one tell a mother that her only son is someone she never really understood, that he's a liar and a larcenist? Yet what else was Karen to believe?

"I think," George began carefully, "that Adela and Stuart are about to make their move to smuggle the mask out of France. That's undoubtedly why they had lunch together in such a fashionable restaurant. After all, for Stuart to have gone there was to invite being recognized by any number of people. He has business contacts here in Paris, people who also go to that restaurant. If he risked being recognized, shooting down the theory that he had disappeared, I think that they're ready to get the mask out, then go to London to collect the ransom money."

"But why should they pay it," Karen asked heatedly. "We all know he hasn't been kidnapped! That it's just a ruse!"

George ignored her question, looking at Lady Macloud. "Does your company have offices in Marseilles?"

"Why yes, of course. A great deal of our freighter business is out of that port."

"Karen," George said, "get on the phone and call all the airlines. See if Stuart has booked a flight to Marseilles, and when. In the meantime I'll alert the Highway Patrol to put up roadblocks on all the main roads to Marseilles."

"What about the railroads?" Karen asked.

George shook his head. "It would take too much time to mobilize them, and it's too difficult. We'd almost have to pass out photos of Stuart and ask every porter to be on the lookout for him."

"But what's the point?" Maggie wanted to know.

"If I'm correct, Adela will fly to London tonight or

tomorrow morning. Stuart, in the interim, will go to Marseilles and arrange for a package to be taken aboard 'as a favor.' When's the next tanker heading out, do you know?"

Maggie closed her eyes as if visualizing a shipping schedule. "The *Caroline* is there now, having delivered her cargo of oil to France. She's set to sail on Sunday."

"That gives Stuart plenty of time to show up in Marseilles, pal around with the crew and ask one of them to take the package as a personal favor. Where's the ship headed?"

"She'll put in for a few hours at Lisbon, then sail to Trinidad for two days."

"And after that?" George seemed to tower over them as he asked the question.

"Buenos Aires," Maggie said.

Karen and George exchanged knowing glances. "Have you told Lady Macloud about Adela?"

"Not fully," Karen said.

"Then I think we should," George remarked. "This will prove painful to you, Lady Macloud," he began.

"Maggie," she corrected.

George nodded appreciatively. "What I'm about to tell you will only show Stuart in a worse light than you've already seen, I'm sorry to say."

Maggie lifted her chin proudly, her green eyes flashing. "I'm prepared to hear anything you may have to say, but that doesn't mean I'll believe it. So far there's been no evidence of anything. From the theft to the ransom note . . . my son *appears* to be implicated, but until I have proof, I'll not give an ounce of credence to his guilt."

Karen wished she could hug the woman. Maggie's

words and tone had simply yet firmly conveyed precisely what Karen herself wished she could feel. The man she had met on the train—she could have said the same things about him. The man she had subsequently encountered though—he had instilled doubts within her, doubts she hated but couldn't deny. Still how could anyone have a mother like Maggie and not be a wonderful human being? In a very real sense Lady Macloud was the best testimonial Stuart could have!

George was concluding the theory that Stuart and Adela were in cahoots, and that Stuart would use Macloud Shipping as a means to smuggle out the mask or anything else they wanted. She had listened intently, her eyes narrowing from time to time. "Consequently," George said, "it seems that they have formed a ring. Then, greed being what it is, they decided to capitalize on the news that Stuart had disappeared."

"Which is what would account for Stuart staying away from his regular Paris residence," Karen put in. "Except for me everyone else thinks he's vanished... which gave them a perfect opportunity to try to blackmail you and the earl."

Maggie nodded to herself. "It's very pat, the way you two have worked this through. On the surface it would appear to be a diabolically clever scheme... not to mention highly profitable."

"But you don't believe it," George stated quietly.

"I know my son," she said evenly. "Unless he has lost his mind, the person you're describing just couldn't be Stuart."

Realizing that they had very little time left, Karen let the two of them continue their conversation while she dialed the airlines. She interrupted them, saying, "No reservation under that name."

"He could be using an alias, but I doubt it. No," George said, his brow furrowing, "Stuart just doesn't want to risk the airport scanners. He'll probably drive down with the mask in his luggage, all wrapped like an ordinary parcel."

"He probably still has the rented Renault," Karen said.

George walked over to the telephone. "I checked that out while I was in Tournus and have already given headquarters the license-plate number," he explained, lifting the receiver. "They'll have roadblocks up within the hour."

Lady Macloud rose to her feet regally. "Then I may as well take my leave," she said. "I'm staying at the George V if you need me. Right now I'll only be glad when you've located Stuart so I can rest at ease that he hasn't been kidnapped after all." She glanced at Karen sympathetically. "I know you believe he's free," she said as George got off the phone, "but a mother's love is a fiercely protective one."

"I understand," Karen replied.

Maggie offered her hand to George with a wan smile. "You'll call me the moment you've learned anything?"

"Of course," he answered gravely.

Then Maggie turned and embraced Karen briefly. "I'm glad you're still open-minded about Stuart. I'd very much like us to be friends once this nightmare is over."

Both Karen and George watched her as she opened the front door and left the apartment with pose and dignity. "She's quite a woman," George remarked admiringly.

"I'll say."

"I—well, I have to ask you to perform a task, Karen, much as it goes against my better judgment."

She glanced up at him, wondering what he was leading to.

"You raised a very good point a little while ago," he said, resuming his seat in the armchair. "You are the only person—outside of Adela—who *knows* that Stuart is alive and free."

Karen sat down on the edge of the sofa and waited for him to continue.

"I want you to go to the apartment on Avenue de Verdun and see what you find out about Stuart's plans. Any hint—whether in word or deed, or even if it looks as if he's beginning to pack a few things—might prove of invaluable aid in solving this crime."

She gasped in surprise. "But under what pretext?" she asked. "How can I explain to Stuart that I know where he lives? If he thinks I've been spying on him, almost anything could happen!"

George frowned. "I know. Worse, because you are the only witness to his whereabouts since the train accident, he may just decide you're expendable. What I'm asking you to do is potentially very dangerous," he said soberly.

"But George—"

He raised his large hand and stopped her. "We'll have to come up with a valid reason to explain how you learned where he was."

"From Adela? Do you think he might believe that?"

He nodded. "As I recall, you told Stuart that I was a retired police detective, didn't you?"

"Yes, during dinner on the train."

"I think you may as well use both approaches. Tell him Adela threatened you unless you stayed away from him—that will appeal to his ego. But it couldn't hurt to add that as a result you asked me to track him down."

"No, that would never do," she said. "His official residence is at the Parc Monceau.... How do we know that he's rented that other place under his real name? I'd be tripped up instantly. Let's stick with Adela giving me the information."

"But why should she?"

Karen shrugged. "I tricked her into it," she suggested. "But my biggest concern is how to get him to confide in me."

"All right, then let's do this. You and Adela had a confrontation, and you managed to get his address out of her. In the meantime I've confided in you that we're close to solving the case, and you've gone to warn him to save his own neck. Tell him you love him—tell him anything you want but find out what he's up to! I'll have a squad car parked nearby, Karen. If he tries anything funny, our men will be in his apartment before you can be harmed!"

"How will you know what's going on inside?" she asked. "Besides, what if he calls Adela to confirm what I'm saying?"

George smiled confidently. "Her line will be 'temporarily disconnected,' and the department will have a bug in his apartment before the night is out."

"Then this is to take place tomorrow?"

"It must. First thing in the morning. I wish we could pull it off tonight, but we'll need the time to have Adela's telephone service disconnected and to plant our bug."

Karen groaned softly. "What can I tell the Kleimers? They'll be furious with me if I'm absent again tomorrow!"

"Let me take care of that," George advised. "I'll pay them a call before I head back to St. Ouen this evening. They'll understand. If you're brave enough to be our decoy in this matter, they should be big enough to overlook a little absenteeism. After all it's your boss who wants the mask recovered—that's what he's paying me for!"

She stared at her foster father. He was no longer the big, burly man she had known most of her life. George Ferrier was once again a police detective in charge of his case and deadly serious. Karen had never seen this side of him, and he was frighteningly formidable. "Do you think this plot will work?"

"It has to—otherwise he may try to kill you!"

Chapter 14

The next morning was overcast, and a light drizzle fell on the rooftops of Paris. Karen hadn't needed her alarm clock; she had not really slept the entire night. Instead she had been filled with misgivings about her assignment. She felt as if she were betraying Stuart...or, more importantly, Lady Macloud. If Stuart was guilty of everything they suspected him of, then whatever happened to him was only just.

But when Maggie found out that she had been instrumental in trapping Stuart...Karen knew the woman would never forgive her. For a moment the previous evening Karen had reacted to Maggie's staunch faith in her son...almost able to agree with her that Stuart couldn't possibly be guilty. But during the night as Karen turned the evidence over and over in her mind, she had reverted to her previous thinking. Just too many undeniable clues pointed to Stuart's definite complicity. Her only hope—and it was a frayed thread—was that phone call to Maggie, telling his mother to get in touch with her. But that, too, could have been part of the plot to make it seem as if he had really been kidnapped.

As the first rays of the sun filtered through her small bedroom window, Karen kicked off the covers and went to the kitchen to put the kettle on. Her eyes were heavy and her mouth felt dry, and she didn't know how she would get through the morning's charade. Luckily she didn't believe Stuart truly capable of violence, or she would have been terrified to go to his apartment. Bugs and waiting squad cars to the contrary it didn't take long for a person to be killed!

Moments later she had showered and was pouring milk into her steaming tea. Then, taking the cup with her, she stood before her closet, trying to decide what to wear. Pants, of course, in case she had to make a run for it; boots for the same reason. But should she strive for a waiflike look, a desperate woman trying to save the man she loved, or . . . ? Ultimately she settled on a pale blue sweater that would bring out the color of her eyes, and navy blue pants. A silk scarf in subtle shades of blue would complete her outfit.

That decided, Karen went back into the bathroom to put on her makeup. Not too much—just enough for effect. Then she caught her reflection in the mirror and, startled, she gazed at herself as if at a stranger.

Her features hadn't changed. There was the straight, rather short nose; the full, wide mouth; the blue eyes beneath the level blond eyebrows. It was in the eyes, she thought . . . whatever "it" was. Something about her expression. A wariness; yes, that was it. A scant ten days had passed since she had met Stuart on the Trans Europe Express, but the woman she saw in the mirror now was different. The tendency to trust people implicitly...the openness...those traits were no longer reflected in her eyes. Instead she saw caution there, an automatic skepticism.

Karen didn't like what she saw. Was she altered because she had wanted to fall in love with Stuart and had been so badly disappointed? Or was it because, on the heels of Alex walking out on her, the first man she'd been attracted to seemed no better...if indeed not worse. Either way Karen now saw that she had—in the purest sense of the word—lost her innocence. The emotional effects of misjudgment and hurt had taken their toll. *It's part of growing up,* she thought, a little sadness mixed with determined pride. *I have to learn that life is not easy, and that I must fend for myself if I'm to be a mature adult.*

She smiled a little ruefully as she finished applying her mascara. Now was not the time for such speculations. She had a task to perform. Like it or not, only she could reach Stuart; only she could try to find out what he was up to next. No one other than Adela knew where he was, purportedly, and the burden of determining Stuart's plans was squarely on Karen's shoulders. She knew that she should be glad to play a part in bringing a criminal to justice...but Karen's heart wasn't in it. She wished she could wake up and find out that none of it was real; she had never met Stuart Macloud, never been on the train to Nice; none of it had ever happened.

But that was hoping for too much. Mr. Cagliani had been robbed, and the ransom note to Maggie was real.

Walking back into the living room, Karen opened the small hall closet and pulled out her fleece-lined green raincoat and the matching floppy-brimmed rain hat she loved. Then she let herself out and went down the apartment stairs feeling more like a criminal than someone out to catch one.

Karen took the subway from the Place de Clichy, changed to a connecting line at Barbès Rochechouart and got off at the Gare de l'Est. From there it was a very short walk to Avenue de Verdun. Glancing at her watch, she saw that it was nearly half past eight, and she wondered if Stuart would be sleeping in...or halfway packed and ready to leave. Karen also hoped that George's men had done their work well.

As she walked up the dead-end street, she saw that there were a number of cars parked; but if one of them was a police vehicle, she certainly couldn't distinguish it from the others. Just as she was about to enter his building, Karen thought she recognized a hurrying pedestrian, but her glimpse of him had been so brief that she couldn't be sure. In the winter months everyone was bundled up and hurrying to work at that hour, and there was a kind of anonymity about all of them.

The front door of the building wasn't locked, but there were four units in the two-story structure. The mailboxes had nameplates that were well worn, but obviously Stuart hadn't rented the place under his own name.

Karen glanced around and listened. Sounds of breakfast dishes being washed up, of children getting ready for school and smells of lard and sausage, of dankness and mustiness, met her senses. The door directly across from her opened, and a boy of about ten, wearing a cap and a wool scarf, came out and stared at her suspiciously, instantly alert. Karen smiled in an effort to seem friendly. "I'm looking for someone," she said, her voice rising in pitch.

The boy simply continued to stare.

"A gentleman," she went on. "About six feet tall, brown hair, hazel eyes . . . ?"

He blinked, a cagey expression in his far too adult eyes. "Are you from welfare?"

Karen couldn't help a small laugh. "No, nothing like that. I'm his friend."

The lad pursed his lips, weighing her statement, then he lifted his shoulders as if to say it was none of his business anyhow. "You must mean Mr. St. Jacques, the upstairs tenant. He lives on the right-hand side, but he usually isn't out of bed till around ten in the morning."

She ran her tongue across her bottom lip. "I, well, I've got some very good news to give him. I don't think he'll mind if I wake him up. Thank you," she said.

The boy didn't bother to answer. He opened the downstairs front door and ran out into the chilly, drizzling morning.

She turned and started up the worn stairway, painfully aware of the peeling paint on the walls, the carved or written initials. Somewhere in the building a baby began to wail, and the mother screamed at it to shut up. A television set came on with a variety show, while some man was shouting about the high cost of living and couldn't his wife learn to save a few dollars.

The sounds, smells and sights of downtrodden poverty, of despair and hopelessness, seemed to permeate the atmosphere, and Karen couldn't understand how Stuart had been able to stand it there . . . for even a day, much less ten! It was one thing to need a hideout, but to have chosen such depressing quarters was beyond Karen's grasp. It wasn't, after all, as if Stuart had no money.

But as she reached the top and set foot on the landing,

such thoughts flew out of her mind. She raised her
gloved hand to knock on the door and hesitated. How
could she go through with it? Wouldn't Stuart see that
she was lying? She wasn't a trained policewoman. . . .
What was she doing there? "Do you think this plot will
work?" she had asked George the night before; and he
had replied, "It has to—otherwise he may try to kill
you!"

Karen had a strong urge to turn away before it was
too late. While she truly didn't believe that Stuart would
cause her any bodily harm, she dreaded the look in his
eyes when he saw through her little scheme. He would
know that she had betrayed him, and it would show on
his handsome face. Surely George would understand if
she left now before she had to see Stuart's expression of
disappointment.

And then she envisioned Maggie's face when the truth
came out. Why couldn't George simply send in the
police to search the place? Why did she have to be the
decoy? It wasn't fair! *Oh Stuart, Stuart,* she thought,
why couldn't you be the man I thought you were!

But Karen knew there was no way out of what she
had to do. She had given her word, and she was only
too aware of the importance of her role in capturing a
man who had committed larceny, and who was also trying to swindle his own parents out of a fortune.

Biting back her torment, Karen rapped on the faded
and scratched door. She was sure no one else in the
building had heard it, but it still sounded like a volley of
gunfire.

A few seconds went by. She heard muffled scrapings,
then a door being closed. A moment later Stuart's voice
came through the closed door.

"Who's there?"

Her stomach fell, and her hands turned icy as her heart began to pound. "It's me, Stuart," she whispered with a dry mouth. "It's Karen."

"Who?"

Tears were brimming in her eyes as she forced herself to repeat her name a little more loudly. The voice on the other side of the door didn't even sound like the man she knew. He sounded like some kind of thug or fugitive! But when the door opened a crack, Karen knew she had to keep her wits about her, not panic or feel sorry for Stuart. She wasn't his wife or his mother or his judge.... She was acting out a part only because she knew it was the right thing to do—no matter how personally painful.

"Wh-what on earth?" Stuart looked down at her in total disbelief. "How did you find out where I lived?"

"May I come in?" she asked, set in her resolve to carry out this plot.

"Well, uh, actually Karen—it's not really a very good idea right now. I'm in the midst of—"

"It's important, Stuart.... I'm here to save you."

He glanced over his shoulder furtively, then opened the door just enough to admit her. "Look, my place is a mess. I wasn't expecting anyone, see, and...."

Stuart was speaking so rapidly that she almost had difficulty following him. He seemed highly agitated and kept looking beyond her as if she had brought an army. Then he seemed to collect his wits, and a suspicious look came into his eyes. "How *did* you find out where I lived?" he demanded sternly.

Karen removed her hat, shaking her blond hair loose

again as she unbuttoned her coat. "Adela," she said simply, her back to him.

"That's impossible," he replied, an edge in his voice.

She turned to face him then. A sick, pitying feeling knotting in her stomach. Unshaven, a cheap flannel robe hastily put on over frayed pajamas, he looked awful; and his eyes were bloodshot, puffy, as if he had had entirely too much to drink the night before—an assumption attested to by the half-empty bottle of gin resting on the floor next to the tattered sofa.

For the first time since the ordeal had begun, Karen saw Stuart for what he really was—a crook, a man of such low morals that he'd steal from his own family. She realized now as never before that the man she had dined with on the train was a myth! *This* was the real Stuart Macloud! A conniving con artist...nothing more than a fraud.

"No, Stuart," she finally said, "it's not at all impossible. I never mentioned it to you before because I didn't think it was terribly important. But Adela came to your room at the lodge in Tournus just as I was leaving you a note. She tore it up and warned me to stay away from you."

He snorted derisively. "She's one of those hot-tempered Latins; I'm not surprised," he said smugly, as if it was to be expected that women would be possessive about him.

"Well, she came to my apartment last night, and this time she threatened me."

"Adela?" He seemed genuinely surprised. "I know she wants me, but I didn't think she'd go all that far," Stuart said, seating himself with a conceited leer on his lips.

Watching his reaction, Karen could feel only revulsion. "I told her that as long as you weren't married, I could see you as often as I liked."

Stuart nodded, smirking. "Surprised she didn't scratch you bald," he said. "So you wormed my whereabouts out of her while she was too angry to think straight, is that it?"

Since he had volunteered the explanation, Karen simply agreed with it. "But that's not the real reason I'm here."

"Oh?" His watchful expression belied his outward calm.

"After Adela left, I called my foster father to see if there was any way I could have her legally restrained from coming to my apartment."

"Oh, yeah, the retired cop," he said in a tone that indicated he agreed with her logic.

Reluctantly Karen sat down on the grimy chair facing him. "He told me all about Adela," she said slowly, "or shall I call her Iris Calderón."

Stuart's head came up, and he glowered at her for a moment. "Yeah? What else?" he asked guardedly.

Karen took a deep breath, trying to force herself to feel an affection that no longer existed. "I came here to warn you, Stuart. I don't know just how involved you are with her, but the police are closing in on the theft of the mask of Lugalki. I shouldn't be here, as I'm certain you realize. George's information was confidential, for me alone. He doesn't even know that we've met, or that I have any interest in you at all," she lied with conviction.

Stuart's grin was confident, openly lecherous. "I was right the other night, wasn't I, baby—you loved the way I kissed you! You like to be treated rough." He laughed deep in his throat as he stood up and came closer to her. "I can give you what you want, baby—I'm all the man you'll ever need," he said, pulling Karen to her feet. His hands went around her waist, bringing her closer to him.

"Let me go, Stuart," she said evenly.

"Why, baby? You're here, aren't you? You can't deny you want me—why else would you want to warn me?"

"I'm asking you to let go of me," she repeated. "For all I know, the police could be arriving here any moment. You don't think Adela is going to take the blame all alone, do you?"

Stuart shook his head, a look of cunning in his eyes. "She won't say a thing. Besides, as long as I've got the mask, she'll have to keep her mouth shut. The cops can't prove a thing without the evidence, and Adela isn't stupid. If she squeals on me, she loses the mask forever. No, baby, Adela isn't going to say a word," he whispered, twisting his fingers in her hair and drawing her face closer.

He smelled of stale gin and cigarettes, and Karen began to know real fear. Her heart pounded. Where were George's men! Couldn't they hear what was going on? She'd gotten an admission from Stuart. . . . Why didn't they break in and take him?

As his lips bore down on hers, she knew better than to struggle. Her only hope was to have him believe that she was in love with him, wanted him to escape. To fight him would be to admit that she was there under false pretenses! Every inch of her silently screamed to be out of his arms, to be free of him, but she had to submit. . . . Where *were* George's men!

"I think you'd better let the lady go, Pierre."

Stuart released her so quickly she almost fell. He froze in place as if seeing a ghost. "How did you get free?" he muttered, staring at the gun leveled at him.

Karen turned in the direction of the man's voice, her eyes wide, her mouth agape. Somewhere in the recesses of her mind she heard heavy footsteps running up the stairs to the second floor. The door to the apartment was thrown open, and the room was filled with police-men with drawn guns, but Karen could only stare at the man standing in the doorway to the adjoining bedroom.

"But . . .?" She couldn't even articulate the question. The man in the doorway was Stuart Macloud! Or a twin!

Chapter 15

They were all assembled in the Kleimer salon later that afternoon. George Ferrier, Ilse and Franz, Lady Macloud, Karen... and the real Stuart Macloud. Along one wall, where the Louis XVI marquetry side cabinet stood, things had been pushed aside so they could all see the mask of Lugalki in its incredible beauty. Typical of the goldsmiths of Ur, the solid gold mask was decorated with rubies and emeralds, and it gleamed its secrets from centuries before.

Franz had wheeled himself before it, studying it with awe. "I never thought I would live to see it in my own home," he uttered with reverence, putting his arthritic fingers out to caress its workmanship and sheer beauty.

Ilse stood near her husband, her hand resting lightly on his thin shoulder. "Eric should be here soon," she said, then turned to Stuart and Lady Macloud. "He's our expert on authenticity," she explained.

George rubbed his chin thoughtfully. "I thought it would be a good idea to know exactly what we've got before turning the mask over to headquarters," he said. "But the captain will have it soon, and then it will be his responsibility."

Something about George's manner disturbed Karen, but she was still too much in a daze to think about such things. It was all she could do not to take some cleanser to Stuart's face to be sure it was the real person and not another imposter!

Stuart caught her glance and smiled understandingly. "I was thrown from the compartment at the point of impact, but on the other side of the train. I was knocked out cold."

George cleared his throat significantly. "We have his full deposition, Karen. Adela and her accomplice took advantage of the situation to kidnap Mr. Macloud—I mean, the viscount—"

Lady Macloud laughed lightly, beaming at her son, then glancing over at George. "You were correct the first time, Mr. Ferrier."

"Naturally I had no idea that Adela and Pierre were on the train. I only had met Adela as Iris Calderón, and she came to my residence at Monceau with some story about participating in a fund-raising charity for merchant seamen's families. There was something very fishy about her, and I simply told her that I'd take it up with my father when I returned to England. But then I entirely forgot about her."

"We have a full confession from both Adela and this Pierre St. Jacques fellow. She'd gone to his place just to be sure that Pierre really was the dead ringer for Mr. Macloud that she thought," George stated with police-manlike delivery.

"But who is this Pierre?" Ilse asked, crossing over to

take a seat next to Lady Macloud on the satin-covered settee.

"A third-rate actor," George answered. "Apparently Adela saw him in some revue in a nightclub and recognized the similarity at once. Naturally she had seen pictures of Mr. Macloud in the periodicals, but she had to be absolutely certain that Pierre could pull off the impersonation."

Franz tore himself away from the mask and turned his chair to face them. "When you think about it, it was quite a risk. This Pierre person speaks no English at all, much less with a proper accent."

"Which is why he had to stay away from anywhere Stuart might be recognized," Karen reasoned. "Even his own apartment, although I'm sure the receptionist would have given him the keys."

"Right," Stuart said. "When I came to, I was bound and gagged, being driven somewhere in the middle of the night by this man who was my double. Let me tell you," he said, grinning boyishly, "it was a *very* strange feeling!"

"Then Adela went with the others to the lodge while Pierre drove to Nice with Stuart as his prisoner," George put in. "Pierre stole the mask, took Stuart to an abandoned cottage not far from the lodge, then put a bandage around his own head and showed up as a straggler from the accident."

"Thank God they didn't kill you," Karen whispered, still not quite able to believe what had happened.

"But," Ilse asked, a slight frown creasing her brow, "they couldn't have known that there would be an accident, could they?"

"No, that was blind luck," Stuart answered. "The

original idea was to put the blame on me because they had learned about my father being invited to the auction. While the plot wouldn't have worked for very long, still it would have given them time to use Pierre to impersonate me as a means of smuggling the mask out of the country."

"Which is what George had theorized already," Karen said.

"Not really, dear. It was your deduction—I can't take the credit for that part," he added kindly.

"Then why did they kidnap you," Karen asked, turning to Stuart, feeling her color rise. What a fool she had been to think even for a second that the other man could have been Stuart. The gentleness in his gaze, the humor and sensitivity. . . the traits that had first captured her were so lacking in the imposter!

"Because," Stuart said, coming over to where she sat and touching her cheek softly, "I was a bonus. Not only would I be temporarily blamed for the theft, but they could then use me for ransom. Pierre apparently flew over to London on Sunday, and on Monday morning he opened a bank account in my name at Lloyds—thus making sure that our signatures wouldn't differ, and that the bank manager would recognize him. By then he'd taken me to his apartment near the railroad station and had left me in a chair with my hands tied behind my back."

"But however did you manage to telephone me this Wednesday?" Maggie wanted to know.

Karen glanced over at her and saw the devotion and joy in the woman's eyes. Her feelings had not been misplaced, and her faith had been more than vindicated.

Stuart laughed. "Have you forgotten that I served in

Her Majesty's Royal Navy," he answered as if that explained everything. "We learned quite a bit about knots.
I finally untied myself," he said, exposing the rope burns
on his wrists, "took out the gag while Pierre had gone to
buy some gin and quickly put in the call. Then I put the
gag back on and retied my wrists as best I could. There
was no reason for Pierre to double-check the rope as
long as I was in the same position I'd been in when he
left."

"But you could have escaped!" Karen exclaimed, confusion in her blue eyes.

Stuart shook his head sagely. "By then I knew that
Pierre was seeing you. I couldn't take the chance that he
might harm you in order to track me down. They were
clever, I must say," Stuart added. "They bugged our
table on the train and recorded everything we said. At
first they thought they might learn more about security
for the mask—but instead it provided them with an air-
tight alibi. You'd believe Pierre was me because he
already knew the things you'd told me over dinner. No
matter what happened, Adela and Pierre couldn't lose!
They'd have the ransom and the mask neatly on its way
to Buenos Aires on the *Caroline* out of Marseilles."

"So," George said, "when Mr. Macloud heard your
voice in Pierre's apartment, he untied himself again and
grabbed Pierre's own gun."

Just then a light rapping interrupted them, and Eric
Guzman entered the room. "Oh, I'm sorry," he said
politely. "I thought I was expected."

"You are, Eric, we're with friends," Franz said, wheel-
ing out of the way so the mask was in plain view.
"We've recovered the mask, as you can see. What we
need to know now is if it's authentic."

Glancing nervously about the room as if he'd stepped into a pit of vipers, Eric walked over to the mask. No one said a word as he took out a small kit from his inside pocket and performed a few tests on the underside of the mask.

At least five minutes passed without a human sound in the room. Finally Eric straightened, closing his kit. "While I've done only a preliminary job, it would certainly seem to be real," he said.

"Which you knew all along," Franz spat out with disgust. "You hoped to keep me from bidding on the mask with that memo of yours!"

"I don't understand," Eric replied, looking at Ilse.

George stepped toward Eric then, pulling a pair of handcuffs from his hip pocket. "We have the full story anyway, Mr. Guzman. But you were the only one at this gallery, other than the Kleimers, with access to the full list of invitees to the auction at Nice. You knew you wouldn't be able to go, so you tied up with Iris Calderón and enlisted her aid—for a share of the profits, of course." Then he added, "We might never have suspected you if we hadn't seen you leaving Pierre St. Jacques's building this morning."

Eric paled and his face seemed to sag. Then he drew himself up to full height. "I'm the expert," he blurted, saliva gathering at the corners of his mouth. "I'm the one who appreciates beauty—not these fools with their money and their petty commercial minds! *They* don't know how to appreciate beauty—only how to capitalize on it! With the paltry sums they pay me to authenticate art, do you think I'd *ever* be able to own anything so lovely!"

"Come along, Mr. Guzman. We're going to take a ride to headquarters."

And then Eric seemed to panic, his eyes bulging. "I had nothing to do with the kidnapping! That was Adela's idea! I was only interested in...."

George led the babbling man out of the room, closing the door behind them. The others sat mutely, the pathos of the situation overcoming them for the moment....

Stuart took Karen back to her apartment. Together they stood at the open doorway. She looked up at him, once again filled with a sense of excitement and anticipation. Now that the mystery had been solved, there was as much comparison between Pierre and Stuart as there was between a photograph and the real person. Stuart's warmth and charm shone through his hazel eyes as he looked at her.

"I asked you on the train if I could see you again when I was next in Paris, remember?"

"Of course," she answered, tingling at his nearness as she had done that night on the train.

He cupped her chin with his hand and smiled at her tenderly. "My mother has asked me to invite you to come to Hogarth to stay with us for a while. Would you accept?"

Tears came to her eyes as she looked at him, feeling his body heat so close to her. "Oh, Stuart, why do I have the feeling that you're holding something back from me?"

He smiled. "I don't want to frighten you away," he said simply.

"How could you do that?"

"By rushing you, Karen Stockwell. All the time I was

a prisoner, the thought of you was my only sustaining hope. I knew that first night when I walked you back to your compartment that I was already in love with you—I wanted to give you all the time you needed to get to know me. And I only hoped that you'd come to love me in time."

Joy rushed through Karen's body like a surge of electricity, and she threw her arms around his neck. "We have all the time in the world now," she said ecstatically.

"You'll love Hogarth. It's quite beautiful there," he said, holding her close and running his hand down her hair in a soft stroking. "Will you come?"

"On one condition," Karen teased.

"That is?"

"That we fly. . . . I never want to take a train again!"

Laughing, Stuart wrapped her in his arms. "Agreed," he said, then his head bent and his lips met hers in a searching, loving kiss. . . a kiss that was a promise.

MYSTIQUE BOOKS

Experience the warmth of love... and the threat of danger!

MYSTIQUE BOOKS are a breathless blend of romance and suspense, passion and mystery. Let them take you on journeys to exotic lands—the sunny Caribbean, the enchantment of Paris, the sinister streets of Istanbul.

MYSTIQUE BOOKS

An unforgettable reading experience.
Now... many previously published titles are once again available.
Choose from this great selection!

Don't miss any of these thrilling novels of love and adventure!

Choose from this list of exciting

MYSTIQUE BOOKS

Experience the excitement of romantic suspense.
MYSTIQUE BOOKS

COMPLETE AND MAIL THIS COUPON TODAY!

MYSTIQUE BOOKS

In U.S.A.
MPO Box 707
Niagara Falls, N.Y. 14302

In Canada
649 Ontario St.
Stratford, Ontario N5A 6W2

Please send me the following MYSTIQUE BOOKS. I am enclosing
my check or money order for $1.50 for each novel ordered,
plus 59¢ to cover postage and handling.

☐ 33　　☐ 36　　☐ 39　　☐ 42
☐ 34　　☐ 37　　☐ 40　　☐ 43
☐ 35　　☐ 38　　☐ 41　　☐ 44

Number of novels checked @ $1.50 each =　$_____

N.Y. and Ariz. residents add appropriate sales tax　$_____

Postage and handling　$_____.59

TOTAL　$_____

I enclose _____
(Please send check or money order. We cannot be responsible
for cash sent through the mail.)

NAME _____
(Please Print)

ADDRESS _____

CITY _____

STATE/PROV. _____

ZIP/POSTAL CODE _____

Offer expires September 30, 1981.　　Prices subject to change without notice.

103563972